4-87

Winton, Tim.

That eye, the sky

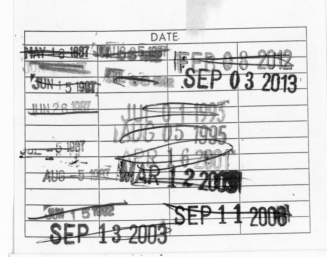

© THE BAKER & TAYLOR CO.

Books by Tim Winton

THAT
EYE,
THE SKY

THAT
EYE,
THE SKY
TIM
WINTON

ATHENEUM   NEW YORK

1987

This novel is a work of fiction. Names, characters, places, and incidents are either the product of the author's imagination or are used fictitiously. Any resemblance to actual events or persons, living or dead, is entirely coincidental.

Library of Congress Cataloging-in-Publication Data

Winton, Tim.
   That eye, the sky.

   I. Title.
PR9619.3.W585T43   1987   823   86-26625
ISBN 0-689-11869-4

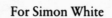

For Simon White

From the otherworld of action and media, this
interleaved continuing plane is hard to focus;
we are looking into the light –
it makes some smile, some grimace.

Les A. Murray, 'Equanimity'

I

Chapter One

Dad has the ute going outside. I am behind Mum. Her dress has got flowers all on it, none of them much to look at. Her bum moves around when she laughs. Dad always says she has a bum like an angry mob which means nothing to me but a lot to him, I reckon. I can hear the rooster crorking out the back. He's a mean rooster – goes for your pills when you collect the eggs.

'Seeyaz.' That's Dad going. He revs the ute up. He's in a hurry, going to town for Mr Cherry.

'Wave him off, Ort,' Mum says to me. She always reckons you should show people you love them when they go away because you might never see them again. They might die. The world might end. But Dad's only going to town for an hour. It's business for Mr Cherry. And there he goes, out the drive and onto the road.

Mum puts her hand on my shoulder and flour falls down my arm. The rooster crorks again. That's a mean rooster. Dad drop-kicks him on Saturday mornings just to let him know who's boss.

'Hop inside and do your homework, Ort,' Mum says.

'In a minute,' I say.

'What you learnin'?'

'Burke and Wills.'

'Uh-huh.'

Mum doesn't know what Burke and Wills is, I bet, but she won't let on. But that's orright. I don't know what it is yet, either. Gotta learn it. That's why it's homework.

'Well, get in there, my second man,' she says, putting up her dress a bit for some air. It's hot.

'In a minute.' I pick at the flap of skin on my stubbed toe. Stubbed toes are something you have to live with in this life.

That mean rooster goes again. I can just see his red dishmop hairdo wickering around all over the place as he yells his lungs off. The sky is the same colour as Mum and Dad's eyes. When you look at it long enough, like I am now with my nose up in it, it looks exactly like an eye anyway. One big blue eye. Just looking down. At us.

My name is Morton Flack, though people call me Ort for short. Ort is also a name for bum in our family. It means zero too (you know, like nought), but in my case it just means Morton without saying all of it. My Dad's name is Sam Flack. Mum is called Alice. Her last name was different when she was a maid. Tegwyn in the next room with her magazines is my sister. She finishes school next month. Grammar lives in the room behind with her piano she never plays. She never does much these days. That flamin' rooster going again.

The light slants down funny on my desk from the lamp Dad fixed up there on the wall. I should be doing Burke and Wills. They don't seem very bright blokes. Instead I'm listening to the night coming across from the forest – all small sounds like the birds heading for somewhere to stay the night, the sound of the creek tinkering low when everything gets quiet, the chooks making that maw-maw sound they do when they're beginning to sleep all wing to wing up under the tin roof of the chookhouse. Sometimes in the night I can hear their poop hit the ground it's so quiet. Sometimes it's so quiet, Dad says you can hear the dieback in the trees, killing them quietly from the inside. At night the sky blinks at us, always looking down.

The sounds of night aren't really what's keeping me from Burke and Wills, though. It's Dad. He's not back. But I'm not worried.

Fat Cherry is my best friend. He's got a head like a potato, eyes like a baby pig's, and his belly shimmies all over the shop when he walks. Until we got separated, Fat and me sat together in school. His real name is James, but even Fat is better than that. Fat Cherry is a good name all round. So's Ort Flack. All the other kids in the district have got names like Justin and Scott and Nathan and Nicholas which are piss-poor in anyone's book. And no kid wants to be called Mary or Bernadette if he's not a girl. Even my chook (my private chook – my pet one) has got a better name than the kids at school. Errol is my pet chook's name. Mum says it's a sacrilege but I haven't figured that out yet. When Errol was a chick I found him outside the chookrun with his leg all busted up and caught in the wire. I put tape on his leg and kept him in bed with me for a week until Mum went off her face about the sheets.

Wait . . . wait on . . . I can hear a car. No, it was someone passing. Someone leaving the city. If you climbed the dying jarrah trees down there towards the creek, you'd see the lights of the city. From here, the only lights in sight are from Cherry's roadhouse a hundred yards along the highway on the other side of the road. You can see their bowsers glowing, and sometimes you think you can actually see the numbers rolling in them, but you're just kidding yourself.

The tail lights of that car burn the bush up and go slowly out. Burke and Wills.

Ah, another car. That'll be the old man. He's late. Boy is he late. Mum'll be mad.

The car comes up the long drive towards us, but the engine noise is all wrong. Mum is going out. If I could, I'd go out too, but I'm all stuck, like the chair has hold of me. I'm scared, a bit. I am scared. I'm scared. There's fast talking out there. *Isn't anyone gonna turn that engine off?*

'Morton? Morton!' Here she comes, setting all the floorboards going, there she is, my Mum, with those eyes full up and spilling, the dress shaking enough to shed all those dumb flowers off it.

The big, strange car shoots us down the driveway and out onto the sealed road with Mum and me rolling across the big back seat that farts and squeaks under us. Headlights poke around in the dark. A man with a bald moon at the back of his head is driving and talking – both too fast. My belly wants to be sick. Mum's eyes are making me wet.

'How far, Mr . . .'

'Wingham, Lawrence Wingham,' the man pants.

'How far?'

'A couple of kilometres, only a couple.'

The speedo is like a clock gone mad. I don't know why, but I feel like I just swallowed a whole egg, shell and all. I can tell something bad's happened – I'm not stupid – but no one has told me yet. I don't know. If my Dad is dead, we just won't live anymore.

The moon sits over the road like a big fat thing. It looks useless as hell tonight. I never felt that about the moon before. As the road goes downhill I can see the pale lights of the city far away. Trees hang all over the road.

'Where's Tegwyn?' I ask.

'She's home looking after Grammar.'

'I could've done that.'

'I want you . . . with me,' she says. I know she's crying. All the door handles glow in the dark. It's like I can see her face in them and she's crying in all of them. Tegwyn will hate looking after Grammar.

Now the road is winding down towards Bankside, the place where my school is. There's two shops, a pub, a bowser, a big church place, and a post office as well. It's not as big as the city.

The orange light makes me jump. I can see it through the trees and it gets stronger as we round the bend. Mum's arm is around me, pushing all the air out of me. A tow truck. Some cars on either side of the road. A big mess in the bush. The flashing light makes the road and the ground and the bush jump. It makes the men walk in jerks.

No one even looks at us when we pull up. Mum is out and running. Dad's ute is all pushed back on itself something horrible. I can see Ted Mann from the Bankside Garage shouting at Bill Mann his brother. It's their tow truck making the orange light. There's not much for them to tow. I stay in the car. Mum has Ted Mann by the singlet. They shout.

'The ambulance has been and gone,' he says.

'When?'

'Ten minutes ago.'

'Tell me, tell me.'

'What, Mrs Flack?' Ted Mann does not like us because we work for Mr Cherry who is competition.

'Is he alright?'

'Looked pretty bloody crook to me,' he says, turning back to Bill Mann to keep up the argument. They're always arguing. Their wives went away to live in the city. Or so Tegwyn says.

I'm all sick. But I can see alright. I'd be sicker if Dad was dead. I know he's not. I know it. But I feel sick enough.

The man in front of me, the man who has driven us here with his bald moon of a head coming up out of the seat, is still here. Mum comes back to the car.

'Can you take me into the city?' she asks the man who starts the big car again.

'That's where I was headed in the first place,' he says, moving around on the seat.

She gets in front with him and then twists around to me. 'You get a lift back with Mr and Mr Mann. I won't be back till late. You've got school tomorrow.'

'School? Mum!' I can't believe it.

'You've got one week of term left. You've never missed a day yet and you're not gonna. If you start something, you finish it. If I'm not back before morning, you get a lift in with Fat and Mr Cherry. Tegwyn will cut your lunch.' She kisses me on the nose hard enough to make me eyes fog up.

Outside the car, there is the dry smell of wild oats and the brown smell of the paddocks and the talk of Ted and Bill Mann. I get in their truck. The big car pulls out and passes and I see Mum wave and fix her hair. Her hair is the colour of white wood. Ted and Bill Mann argue. I get out because it's hot in the cab. Ted Mann looks at me and shrugs.

Dad's ute is so small. I look inside. The seats are all back and forward and up and over everywhere. Everything inside is sticky. It's blood – I'm not stupid. I go round the side to where the open tray is. A bale of hay has come loose and spilt itself all over. There's his big tool box still there, and on it, the big rag that he wipes his hands on. It used to be a pair of my pyjama bottoms until the bum came out. I pick it up. It smells of turps and oil and

[7]

grease. It smells of my Dad. A long way away there is a siren. That will be the police. It's a long way for them to come. I suppose they will look at the skid marks and those trees over there that are all flat and sprinkled with glass.

Mr and Mr Mann are arguing about how they'll tow the ute. I stand here waiting. The sky blinks down at me.

Chapter Two

In a couple of years they're going to pull this school down. It's only a tin shed, so it won't take much. Next year I have to go to high school in the city anyway. That means I'll get home at six o'clock like Tegwyn; six o'clock when there's only three hours of light left – and that's in summer. High school. I don't like thinking about it. Tegwyn's been there three years and she *still* doesn't like thinking about it. Funny to think this school will be gone. Bankside used to be the country. Now you can see the city at night. Soon the city will be here.

Across the classroom I can see Fat. He's trying to get me to look at him. One little pig eye winks, and I want to wink back but I can't. He keeps winking a message in morse code but I can't even look properly at him. His Dad was all strange in the truck this morning when he gave us a lift. Tegwyn kept looking at me as we twisted down the hill in low. Mr Cherry didn't say a word. Sometimes he drives us nuts with his talk and showing us his funny eyes, all black and shadowy. He says he looks like Eddy Canter whoever that is. Bores us dead. But today not a word. When the truck bumped around and I hit my head on the door, he gave me a funny look as if to say 'Don't even say ouch or I'll dump you out on the side of the road'. Tegwyn burped then and giggled and Fat got a clip on the ear as if *he* did it.

Mr Cherry isn't very big. He looked even smaller this morning, as if the steering wheel had grown. He hadn't shaved and his chin was full of little grey iron filings like the ones on his workshop floor. He didn't say one word about my Dad.

'James! James Cherry.' Mrs Praktor has seen Fat's spastic winking. Praktor-the-tractor. Good ol' Max Factor. That's what we always say. 'Sit up straight and do your work.'

Someone giggles. Someone always giggles. There's all grades in this class. It's the only class in the school. Nathan Mann is year six. Bernadette Mann is year four. Mary Mann is year four, too. Bernadette and Mary are twins, but you wouldn't know it. One like a horse, one like a camel. Billy Ryde is only year two. There's all grades, but me and Fat are the only year sevens.

It's hot in here. You can hear the bush moving around outside like it's tossing and turning in the heat.

At lunch Fat and I play french cricket under the big tree with the bits of lumpy lawn under it. I keep chipping the ball away near his feet and when he dives for it, his whole belly goes nuts.

'Have you heard about my Dad?' I say, knocking one a bit too high.

He snatches the ball.

'Gotcha.'

'Made it easy for you.'

'Ah yeah.'

'Did ya hear anything?'

'Carn, gis the bat.'

'Well?'

He takes the bat and faces up. Across the yard the Mann twins are playing skippy. Their plaits jump around like propellers. They look like they're gonna take off any moment. Chuck-chuck-chuck, a camel helicopter and a horse helicopter chopping across the paddock, over Mann's Garage and the Bankside Arms down towards the city. I take the ball. It's a furry old six-stitcher Fat's Dad gave him. I put it at him high on the bat and Fat jumps back out of the way.

'Well?' I say, grubbing in the lumpy grass for the ball.

[10]

'My Dad told me not to talk about it.'

'Don't then.' I throw low and he hits sideways and I miss the catch and I'm angry all of a sudden.

Errol and me sit out on the back verandah. His beak is all hooky and busted. His eyes are pink. The way he looks at me, sometimes, you wouldn't know he was a chook. My schoolbag is all hot and leather-smelly from being in the sun. I toss Errol across the verandah and he garks and fluppers and I go inside to the cool of the house.

'Is that you, Lil Pickering?' Grammar calls out.

'No, jus' me, Grammar.'

She makes mumbly, spluttery noises and then goes quiet. As I pass her door I look in. There she is with her feet up on the window sill and the breeze up her nightie.

'Lil Pickering?'

'No, just Ort, Grammar.'

In her hand there's a big red apple. She likes to have things like that around, bright things she can still see. Sometimes she just looks at her feet which are the colour of boiled crayfish and stink twice as much. Old people are a bit boring and a bit scary. But I go in because something makes me. And there she is, all tears down her face, big branches of them. You'd think they were our family tree. Her arms are all old and bag down under. I just shine her apple with me hanky and leave our family tree on her face and go out.

There is a bit in me, you know, that tells me my Dad is not dead. But it isn't enough. Fat won't come over to muck around today – I just know it. I don't want to muck around anyway. I'm just sitting here in the cool kitchen thinking of all the things I don't want to do. It only takes one thing to make you unhappy.

I should go down to the old sawmill. I should be thinking of all the funny things that have happened to us. I should chop some kindling and start the fire for Mum – Tegwyn will be home in a minute. I should . . . I should figure out why all . . . Mum's glass jars along the shelf above the stove are all full of . . . jewels. Crikey! In the flour jar there's big red stones like the big lumps you get with a blood nose. And in the rice jar there's diamonds! Eight big, fat jars with their lids pointing at me, all full of shining things. Jewels!

'Oh, Ort.' There's Mum standing in the doorway with her arm against the frame. Her hair is across and up and all over the place and her eyes are red. 'Thought you might get the stove going for us.'

I don't say a word. I've still got one eye on those rubies and gems. I point at them. Mum looks and then looks back at me.

'What?' she whispers.

And then they're gone. Flour and rice and lentils and icing sugar and tea are back in their jars.

'No. Nothin'.'

Mum looks at me and I look at Mum.

'Is that you, Lil Pickering?' Grammar calls from down in her room.

'No, Mum, it's me,' Mum calls. 'Come on, Ort, get the stove going. Tegwyn'll be wanting her bath.'

'Is Dad dead?' My mouth just says it – I can't help it.

'No,' she says, tying an apron on, the one with Sydney Harbour Bridge on it. 'No, he's not dead.'

'Is he crook?'

'Pretty crook, yes. He's in a coma, Ort. He's not awake. In a coma. Like you were once. You probably don't remember.'

But I do remember. I was only small, but I do remember. I was dead. Twice. Two times my heart stopped and my brain stopped.

'You had meningitis. Your head was all full of water. You screamed like you were on fire. And then you went asleep and didn't wake up for two weeks.'

I remember. It was like a sea, up and down on waves and the light was like after the sun has just gone down, and voices called.

'Twice, you know, they said it was all over. But I didn't listen to them and neither did you. In hospitals you just don't listen to them 'cause they don't know any better than us. They don't really know what it is that makes people work. They just guess.

'In the end there was me and these three nurses – rebels they were – and we just kept talking to you, talking about the weather and how's yer father –' she stops for a moment and I look at me toe-scabs – 'and the doctors went crook and tried to keep us away.

He can't hear you, they said. But we just kept on chatterin' away there until one morning you just woke up. You were a baby all over again. You were born all over again. Had to have you in nappies. Three years old – in nappies. God, I cried.'

All of a sudden Mum is at the sink doing absolutely nothing at all except having her shoulders jump up and down.

'I remember,' I say to her.

'Your father'll remember too. When it's all over, he'll remember.'

I don't sleep that good. Never have. Even when I was little and Mum or Dad put me to bed, I'd lie awake until they'd gone to bed themselves – longer even. It's lonely in the middle of the night with just you and the sky and the noises of the forest. There's no one to talk to except that big sky. Sometimes I talk to it. Sounds funny, but I do. Ever since they brought me home from the hospital the time I was so sick, I haven't slept good. It's like those two weeks of sleeping in the coma were enough sleep for one person in their life. Strange to think that Dad's down there in a hospital in the city asleep, hearing all those voices and seeing all those colours like I did. He won't sleep much good when he gets better, that's for sure. Still, he's not much of a sleeper anyway.

I can hear Tegwyn talking in her sleep. All night she was playing Grammar's piano. She hammers up and down on it with her brown plaits hanging down forward, her long fingers going at it like mad, her back bent like a slave. She bashes that piano, Tegwyn. I don't know about her. Sometimes I see her in the shower through the hole in the asbestos. She sings to herself. She's got big boobs – they look like pigmelons – bigger than Mum's. Mum's are like two socks full of sand. Tegwyn isn't happy much. When she's in the shower she soaps her legs and in between like she's trying to hurt herself. She looks at her soapy brown legs with a sad look. And sometimes she looks straight into the shoot of water that comes out of the shower head. She lets it go right into her eyes. For a minute, sometimes, looking straight into it and letting it hurt her. I don't think she feels it until she goes to sleep. That's why she groans and calls out in her sleep. Those noises make me cry for no reason, sometimes. Night time is like that. Crazy things happen and you just can't help it.

I was born at night. In this house – out in the livingroom. Mum and Dad talk about it now and then. It was winter and cold. Dad said he could hear a dog barking somewhere all night. Mum was all fat with me inside and in those days there wasn't any ute. The people who owned Cherry's Roadhouse in those days had a car, but they were out seeing people in Bankside. Mum started to hurt with me, and Dad put her in the livingroom where the fire was going hot and red. All the time he was looking through the curtains across to the roadhouse to see if the people had come back with their car. There was no phone. Still isn't – Mum and Dad don't like them. It was a long drive into town and the hospital. Dad was starting to get jumpy. Mum said he kept stoking the fire up for something to do until the room got so hot that the wallpaper started to come off. Then Dad was running around trying to put the wallpaper back up and while he was doing that Mum had me on the sofa and the first thing I must've saw was those lousy brown flowers on the sofa and my Dad chucking a mental.

Mum said I came out all blue with that cord thing all round me neck. She bit it. Ugh! And pretty soon I went all pink and she gave me some milk from her boobs which probably weren't so socky in those days. Well that's what Tegwyn says.

I've always lived in this house – even from the first day. Maybe that's why I like it so much. Tegwyn was born in hospital. I know enough about hospitals to tell you that you don't want to be *born* in one.

Mum was born in a truck coming across the Nullarbor Plain. She just got shook out. The Nullarbor has the worst roads in the world. Dad got born on the enquiries desk of a police station. He says they just cut his cord and put him in the OUT basket. Grammar used to talk about it once. I think she was born on a farm up north where all the ground is red and it rains in summer and is warm in winter.

Being born is hard work. Mum says people scream. Errol came out tapping. His egg just opened up and there was no screaming, but I suppose it was hard work all the same.

People die, too. Even stars die – you see them falling out of the sky. Mum used to say it was the sky shedding a tear.

Tegwyn is asleep now. Everything is asleep.

Before I go to sleep, I go out and pee off the back verandah. The ground smells summery. That stupid rooster is at it. Middle of the night. A long time after I'm dried up, I stand out there looking up to see if maybe a star might fall.

Chapter Three

The summer holidays came so quick – here they are. I'm in them! And here I am with Fat, walking along the top bank of the creek down towards the sawmill with everything jumping in the trees, and the pods snapping and popping in the heat. I've got one eye out for snakes and the other out for something different. Down here, you always find something different. Holidays do that to you, you know. You see better, you smell better.

In the reeds along the edge of the creek, frogs churk and gulp and catch flies. The water is still and brown. By the end of summer there'll probably be no water at all and there'll be roos and rabbits sniffing out pools all along here at dusk. Tadpoles scribble away across the surface. Birds tip-toe here and there like old ladies. There's tigersnakes about, but you just don't think about that.

'Can you see it?' I ask Fat. His shirt is off and his bellybutton is full of flies. Fat squints. When he moves, his bellybutton squints too, but those flies won't move for anything.

'Nup.'

'Should be along here somewhere. Was 'ere in winter. 'Member that time you nearly drowned us?'

'That was your fault.'

'Ah, pull the other one.' Fat capsized us. I can't say anything. He knows he's fat – he doesn't need me to tell him.

'There,' Fat says, 'there it is.'

We run along for a bit and then edge down the bank on our bums to where we can see the brown corner of that car roof we had last summer.

'It's pretty rusty,' I say. We try to pull it out. Grass and pigface have grown all over it and it's half-buried in mud. There's even roo poop on it. But there's no holes in it, and pretty soon we've got some long sticks for poles and we're out on the water. The creek is only six foot wide or so, but it's deep in places. After pushing away and making a lot of noise – what with shouting at Fat to keep in the middle, and nearly losing my pole – we get going smooth and quiet and the only noise is the water moving aside to let us pass and the mosquitoes playing their sirens all around.

When it's like this, and you're doing something quiet with someone, like when Dad and me are walking through the forest, or when Mum and me have stopped reading a book together 'cause it's started to rain all of a sudden, it's then that you feel like you know what both of you are thinking and you don't have to talk. Fat's back is pink already from the sun. I can hear him breathing. He hasn't been over for a while. We've done some things, me and Fat.

'Mum an' Dad had a fight las' night.'

I look up from the water. He talked.

'Yeah?'

'Mum kep' hittin' 'im with the *Sunday Times*.'

I laugh. The *Sunday Times* is what Dad used to hit his dog with, before the dog got caught in a rabbit trap and had to be put down.

'He was . . . cryin'.'

'Oh.'

Fat steers us away from the end of a log all clotted with ants. I don't say anything.

'Like a baby.'

We keep poling quietly down the creek until we get to the sawmill.

For a long time they cut the forest up at the sawmill. Down around Bankside you can see stumps everywhere, little grey toadstools. All the farms in the district used to be forest. Now the forest is only this small bit behind our place and along the main

[18]

road for a mile or so. It goes down to the edge of the scarp – another mile – and that's all. And now there's dieback eating them all to death. My Dad talks about it a lot. He loves trees. He had a fight with a logger once, but that was a long way before my time and Mum reckons it's not true anyway. The sawmill hasn't been used since I've been alive – that's twelve years. We pull up near it, and shimmy up the bank.

Fat and me kind of stand around, picking through things, but our hearts aren't in it. I climb into what's left of the old furnace and shout. My word jumps back at me and goes across and up in an echo: You!   You!
          You!
Everything is rusty and when you touch it it falls apart or makes your hands red. The sheds are all falling over. Some saws are still left, but you couldn't move 'em with an earthquake. There's big wheels and cogs and pistons, but nothing fits together anymore. Possums live up under the roof. They must get used to the flapping tin. It wasn't such a good idea to come here. Everything is too sad.

'Why were they fighting?' I ask Fat as we push further downstream. Flies and mozzies divebomb us. Something crunches off into the bush. 'Your Mum and Dad.'

Fat doesn't say a word. He hardly moves. Maybe he's trying hard to keep balance. His pink legs come out either side of him like wings.

We float on down, pushing ourselves over logs with our poles bleeding sap where we broke them off.

He doesn't say a thing.

Where the creek meets the main road, there is a wooden bridge with white rails and big black piles driven into the bank at either side. Sometimes Fat and me like to lie under there in the cool with all the insects singing and listen to the cars going across, setting all the boards going like a xylophone. There's a high note at one end, and a low one at the other. Cars come up the scales or down them. Tegwyn says it's not real scales at all and we're jus' kids. Fat

[19]

usually makes a fart with a hand under his arm and that makes her go away. 'I'm so disgusted,' he'll say, walking after her the way she walks with her bum going from side to side.

As we get far enough around the bend to see along the high banks, Fat says:

'There's someone under there.'

'Who?'

'How do I know?'

'Let's get out and go over, see who it is.'

'No,' Fat whispers, 'it's quieter on the water. Let's float down closer. They won't see us if we keep to the bank.' He's right, you know. He's not dumb, Fat.

From behind a fallen log, we watch the person under the bridge. I can hear Fat's heart. Small birds wink past. It's a man. Older than my Dad. His pants are grey and baggy. He's on his knees with his hands in his lap and his head is all back so that his black hat kind of hangs off and looks like it'll fall any moment. Sometimes he looks like he's talking because his mouth moves. Beside him is a blanket and a little brown bag. Fat looks at me and I look at Fat.

A car, a station wagon, rushes over and sets the bridge xylophoning up the scale but the man on his knees under the bridge doesn't seem to hear.

'He's been sleepin' here,' Fat says, very quiet. We're close enough to hit him with a stone, an easy underarm throw. His face is brown and looks like the old saddle Dad has out in the shed – all cracks and lines that change when his lips move. His teeth are very white. His hands are big in his lap. He looks clean enough. Suddenly he reaches behind and pulls up a head of grass and squeezes it in his hands until all the soil falls away, then he just holds it to his face and his lips keep moving.

We sit here for a while, hardly breathing, not taking our eyes off him for a minute.

The sun is almost down by the time we get over to Fat's place, and in the driveway of the roadhouse there is a man in a Ford flat-top with the horn going on and off and his face all red above a shirt and tie that are both undone as if he's been tearing at them he's so angry.

'How the bloody hell does a man get some service around this godforsaken place?' he's yelling between honks.

'How much do you want?' Fat says, his eyes going thin very quick. He pulls the nozzle off the bowser and takes it over to the Ford. 'Your petrol cap's locked.'

'Leave it alone, Slim. I want your father.'

'You won't fit him in there,' Fat says, pointing to the petrol tank.

The red man with the pulled tie and open shirt says to me: 'You think that's funny?' His eyes are white on his face. He looks like he might open the door and climb down any moment.

'No, sir,' I mumble.

'How much do you want?' Fat asks again. He looks like nothing could make him laugh. But his belly gives him away; I can see it just beginning to shuffle around.

The man puts his sunglasses on and looks like he's going to do something any moment. Then he's leaning forward a little – going for the door handle. No, he's winding the window up. The bowser rumbles. Fat points the nozzle onto the truck's tray. With a sharp kick the Ford starts up. The man looks at me for a second and then he drives off with a squeal. I can't believe it. And there's petrol pouring off the tray as he swings out onto the road and heads down towards the city. Pouring off. Like the back of a council water truck.

I turn to Fat. He's got this cheesy grin all over him and there's still drips of petrol running down the steel tip of the nozzle. 'Fat!'

And then we're both laughing our teeth out.

For a while we fossick about in the workshop, once or twice putting the hydraulic lift up for a dare. There's a calendar on the back wall from 1969. That was the year after Tegwyn was born. On the calendar there's a girl with big brown boobs and a dumb look. *Pirelli*. Pirelli is tyres. All over the floor there's tools and parts and gobs of oil and bits of rag. This is where my Dad works. Sometimes I come in here and see his bum sticking out of the bonnet of someone's car. The radio always plays and there's revving and the chink of spanners. *Y'canna hand a man a grander spanner . . . SIDCHROME.* But it's not so friendly in here with him gone. It's kind of cold and dumb and dirty.

'I better go in,' Fat says.

I nod. I follow him round the side of the house to his bedroom window and give him a boost up. The flywire is all busted. He flops in onto his bed and the springs twang. You can hear Mr and Mrs Cherry yelling in the kitchen.

'Seeya,' Fat says from inside.

'Seeya,' I say, not wanting to go.

'It had nothing to do with me . . .' Mr Cherry is yelling. I can't hear all the words, but I listen as hard as I can. The sun is gone now and the bush is all blue with twilight.

'You work the man . . . and then expect . . . like a bloody errand boy . . . just . . . your little weakness. You're a weak man, Bill Cherry . . . so weak . . . can't even bring . . . admit it. Your bloody gambling will ruin us one day – I said that.'

'Oh, look, the man was an innocent. He . . . liked . . . never said a . . . even offered . . . take the bets in and collect for me. Anyway, he always drove too fast for his own good.'

'. . . about him as if he's something in the past.'

'Well.'

'You're a weak man, Bill Cherry. You use a man so you can save face and all the time he gets the reputation in town of a compulsive gambler . . . me sick. You hear? Sick!'

'. . . said enough.'

'Never.'

'I said that will be all.'

'That poor woman.'

'You never cared a black damn for her.'

'You . . .'

'. . . you . . .'

'You!'

From here I can see our porch light on, getting stronger with the darkness and very softly I can hear a voice calling my name. It's not Mum or Dad, but someone kind of familiar, and anyway it reminds me to stop listening to Fat's privacy.

Mum'll sting me for being so late, but her heart won't be in it. None of us can get our hearts in much, these days.

Chapter Four

Today is my first visit to the hospital and even though it's only ten o'clock in the morning, the noise of Mr Cherry's truck is making me sleepy because I was up before the sun. Honestly, I spent all night trying so hard to be asleep that I woke up more tired than when I went to bed. Today I will see my Dad.

Mum and Mr Cherry don't talk. They haven't said a thing all the way. I want a pee real bad but I am too scared to ask. They look like they might blow up. I just watch the stumps and fences and the billboards and hold on and get dreamy.

This morning I stood out on the back verandah and listened to the birds wake up. The little sleepy, cheepy sound they make is the same sound chickens make under their mum just after they've hatched. I listened till they started to sound like grown up birds and then I went inside to check on everyone. I check on everyone all the time. Fat calls it perving, but it's really just checking on them. I like to see them. To see that they're alright, that they're still the same. This old house is full of holes. The asbestos is cracked and none of the doors fit so it's easy to check on everyone. I just sit and watch for a while.

Grammar was asleep with her lips going rubbery with snores. All her silver hair was on the pillow. When I concentrated, I could make out everything in the room: the dusty piano, all her pictures of Dad and some of Mum and other people I don't know, the dresser with combs and Pop's old medals and yesterday's apple. A swallow appeared on the windowsill and looked in, too. Some breeze moved the curtain at the side and the swallow was gone.

Tegwyn's room was darker, with the curtains drawn. All her walls are crowded with people. It must be like sleeping in a cage in the zoo with all those people watching. Piles of magazines hold each other up under the window. Her bed was all piled with her sheets and her legs, and her hair was like Grammar's all over the pillow except black. Over her sheet, one boob poked its nose. She slept quiet.

Mum and Dad's room is easy to see into. The door handle is missing and the hole is big enough to see just about everywhere inside. Sometimes I wonder about checking on people. That's when I see Mum and Dad without clothes on actually *doing it*. You kind of wish they didn't have to do that, but lots of people do. Fat says he thinks his mum and dad probably do. And other kinds of things do it. You see the drake hissing and chasing one of the ducks, wings smacking around until she gets caught and bashed into the ground and jumped on and all the feathers bitten out of her neck. It's natural, but I don't reckon that's any excuse. At least Mum and Dad only hurt each other in small bits. They make little hurting noises, but pretty soon after that they stop, like they know when they've had enough.

It's hard to watch. And hard to stop. Sometimes I just see them talking to each other. Might be about the day or about Tegwyn and me. I can watch all night when they do that.

This morning it was only Mum asleep with her bum up and her face down. A big white bum that got pink with the sun. A bum like an angry mob (still don't get it). I came out of that bum. Gotta face facts.

Fat reckons it's wrong. Checking on people, I mean. Mostly I reckon it's the best way of making sure you know how your family is getting on. You get looked at all day and all night anyway. That eye of the sky sees you – why worry about your kids or your brother looking? It's honest enough.

Funny, I keep thinking about people getting born and things getting born. Things die, too – I'm not stupid. Grammar will die before long because she's lived a long time and has just about had enough. Chooks die. Forests die. I had a brother once. There are scars like train tracks on Mum's belly. She was big with a baby when I was nine. Dad used to put his face on that big parcel and listen. When it came time to have the baby, she went into hospital in the city and came back a week later with nothing, only stitches and full eyes. I used to watch her squeezing milk from her tits into little bowls. I didn't know what it was all about then. I can't remember everything from that time, but I do remember Mum squeezing milk. And I do remember Dad on the bed when no one was around, crying, crying. I know how Fat feels. It's scary when your Dad cries.

Here I am, half asleep in Mr Cherry's truck with houses and shops going past. Traffic lights, billboards, people out on their front lawns with hoses, cars, cars, cars . . . it's the city alright. And none of us is saying a word.

Here I am mumbling in my head. Here I am on the way to see my Dad asleep in hospital.

I'm glad I live just out of the city. Mum and Dad moved out before Tegwyn and me were born. Dad said he wanted to live near trees. Mum said she wanted to live near Dad. I reckon it's made them happy. The trees all being chopped down made them mad, but even dying trees are trees. I don't know everything about us Flacks. Only what I hear and what people tell me. You spend your whole life trying to work out where you fit.

Here I am.

'Here we are,' says Mum, pointing to a big, long white place smothered in carparks and signs and people with bunches of flowers. 'This is the hospital he's at.'

Mr Cherry says nothing. His dark eyes look even darker today; he seems to be getting smaller. I'm pretty certain now that I don't like him. He makes us feel guilty for being in his truck.

We scoot into one of the driveways and as a toll gate comes down in front of us, Mr Cherry digs into a pocket, but before he comes out with anything, Mum puts fifty cents on the dashboard. He takes it and gives it to the man in the glass box. The gate goes up. We're in.

Zigging and zagging up the bitumen carparks, Mr Cherry finds a space in the end and when he's fitted us in the space, he turns the engine off.

[25]

'I'll wait here,' he says.

'You sure will,' Mum mutters. She opens the door.

It isn't like I remember. This hospital is like the State Government Insurance Office that Dad took me to once: long halls that go nowhere, paintings on the walls that don't make sense, people rushing past without looking at you. No sick people anywhere. We go through a place where everyone is smoking. It stinks. There's music, soft and weak. Lifts bong like clocks. Still no sick people.

'Why didn't Tegwyn come?' I ask Mum, who is walking very fast. Her dress is yellow as a duckling. Her shoes are black and a little bit dusty. When she looks down her hair falls into her eyes which are never the same colour twice.

'Tegwyn came yesterday. She didn't want to come today.'

'Is there something wrong with her, do you reckon?'

She looks at me. Her teeth are straight. 'Ort, I don't know what's right and wrong, sometimes.'

Then we're down another corridor. Down the end on a door it says I.C.U.

'I.C.U.'

'Intensive Care Unit,' she says. 'That's where he is.'

Now my heart is jumping around in me.

'Before we go in, I just want to say something.'

'Yes?' I say, wishing she'd said something all the way down in the truck.

'He looks different to last time you saw him.'

Last time, last time. Geez, it's such a long time ago, since before the start of the holidays. Last time. There he was, kissing Mum on the face and walking out to the ute with no shirt on and his back the colour of red mud. He had shorts on with elastic in the back, the ones that make your hips crinkly. When he got in the ute and looked out, I saw a gob of grease on his chin. His black hair was tied back in a plait. He was smiling. That was last time.

'How different?' I ask.

'Well, he's asleep for a start,' she says with a half-way grin. 'And he's been in a terrible accident, of course, and to help him stay alive the doctors have put tubes in some places for food.'

[26]

'For food?'

'It's called a drip,' she says. 'It's water with . . . things in it that feed him. And . . .'

'What else?' This is getting scary.

'His mouth doesn't look very nice, but that's because he doesn't use it much. He gets ulcers and sores in it. Things like that.'

'Oh.'

'You'll have to be a bit brave.'

'I'm not a baby,' I say, with my own half-way grin. We walk to the door. 'Mum?'

'Yes?'

'What's a compulsive gambler?'

'Someone,' she says, 'someone who gets people hurt.'

I.C.U. Here it is. And in we go.

The room is quiet, oh geez, so really very quiet. A nurse comes up and smiles. She looks real lonely in here. There is a big desk, high like a stage, in the middle of the room. All the walls are glass halfway up. There's beeps and quiet whooshes.

'Mrs Flack.'

'I've brought my son.'

'Only for a moment, then.'

We follow her. My feet are real heavy. It's hard work walking. I can't see into any of the rooms. The glass bit is high. We go in one. Everywhere there's machines like big computers and TV screens.

'Here he is, Ort,' Mum whispers.

'There's some visitors for you, Mr Flack,' the nurse says to a long thing on a table. She smiles at us and goes just outside.

Mum bends down and kisses it. When she moves out the way I can see it's him. His eyes are half open like he's only half asleep. Tubes come out his nose. Down the side there's tubes in his leg and arm. His mouth is all black and horrible. Scabby. Everything stinks of cleaning stuff. Everything is shiny. My Dad looks crowded and small in here.

'Hello, love,' Mum says, 'it's me. I've brought Ort with me. He's come to see you. He's a bit nervous 'cause they cut off your hair.'

That's it! His long plait is gone. His hair is all spiky. Mum brings me in close. I can hear him breathing. His hair. His hair.

'Hello, Daddy,' I say like I'm a baby or something, 'it's me, Ort. You got a nice room here. All computer games. They're gonna make pinball with computers, Fat reckons. Don't think you'll like that, eh? Errol says hullo. I'm going to high school next year. Reckon I'm too young yet. I could stay down for a year, eh?' Mum touches me on the shoulder. 'Well, have a good sleep. But wake up, eh? When yer ready.' Me eyes get hard to see through. 'Well, Dad, over and out.' The nurse comes in and gets us.

Before she goes to bed, Mum comes into my room and sits on my bed. I've been reading a book I read when I was ten. Mum pats the sheet near my leg. Her gown is loose and I can see the edge of one of those socky boobs of hers. Her hair is up like a big knot of pine and she looks kind of sleepy and I can tell she's been doing some hard thinking.

'You were brave today,' she says.

'Didn't need to be. It was still Dad.'

All of a sudden she's up on the pillow with me and putting her arms around me like she used to when I was really a kid. She is warm and her gown is fluffy and her breath smells like cough medicine and my head is on her shoulder looking down into that long dark crack between those bosoms.

'I'm proud of you, Ort. You know I love you.'

'Yes,' I say real quiet. 'I know that.'

'Can you tell me something?'

'Me?' It's a surprise.

'There's something I need to know.'

'What can I tell you?' I feel all silly.

'It's something no one else in the world can tell me.'

And that gets me all frightened and flappy inside.

'You see . . .'

'Yes?'

'Well. What was it like when you were asleep in that coma when you were so little? Maybe you don't remember – I don't s'pose you do – but I need to know real bad. Can you remember any little thing? You see, people talk, they say all kinds of things, they give you pamphlets and forms to sign until you don't know your bum from a mineshaft, and . . .'

'I remember,' I say, before she starts to cry properly. 'I remember.'

[28]

'Were you alive?'

'Course. Course I was alive.'

'But inside your head. In your sleep. Did you think things? Did you hear things?'

'Yeah, I heard things, I saw things.'

'Because some people say your father's not really alive.'

'He's alive. He isn't dead!'

'Hush a bit. You'll wake Grammar up.'

I feel really messed up. I pull my book out from under her leg; it's all crumpled.

'What you reading?' she asks, sniffing.

'It's about some kids who go into a weird kind of land through a wardrobe. It's a Poms' book. The kids are wet and they talk funny, but . . .'

'But what?' She picks the book up and bends it back into shape.

'It's not really all that make believe. Things happen.'

'What things?'

'Crazy kinda things. You hear things sometimes. See things. You think sometimes you're somewhere else.'

'In dreams, you mean?'

I look around the room, at my leaning wardrobe, the picture of Luke Skywalker, at the bits of wood I keep because they look like animals and stuff, the plane Dad made me out of balsa, and then I look at Mum and see her worried face.

'What if they're not dreams? What if you're awake when you go to sleep and dreaming when you wake up?'

'What if, eh?' She smiles. 'I dunno, Ort. I just don't know about that. I can't even get me mind to think about it. Maybe it's all the same thing.'

I shrug. Maybe it is. I don't even know what we're talking about anymore.

'Is Dad coming home?'

'Yeah, he's coming home.'

'When?'

'When he's good and ready. He only ever does things when he's good and ready.'

'He's not dead.'

'I'll tell them that.'

She kisses me on the cheek and goes, walking a little bit wonky.

[29]

Out on the back verandah I can hear something moving around in the grass down past the back fence. Could be a fox or a roo or anything. The sky is very clear tonight. Kind of the same colour as my Dad's poor mouth. Stars look like they're moving and still at the same time.

The wind makes a kind of noise in my ear that reminds me of a bell. Not a school bell. Deeper. Bong, in my ear. It makes my toes tingle.

A word slips out of my mouth.

'Please?'

Chapter Five

Tegwyn and me are walking into Bankside this morning because it's Saturday. I don't know why we go in on Saturday mornings. We've been doing it for years. We just do. Because it's hot as hell out in the sun, we stick to the shade of the forest edge which makes walking harder with all the logs and holes and bushes to get past, and the snakes to look out for, but it's not as bad as having your brain casseroled by the sun out near the road. A lot of the time Tegwyn walks in front of me – it's to save talking. Her hair is back in a big, long bready plait that flaps against her shirt. The plait comes down to my eyes; that's how tall she is. She's as big as a grown up woman. Her pink shorts grab her bum and push out half moons at the edges. Sweat all runs down her legs. The flies paddle in it.

Birds crash through the treetops and now and then a car goes past out on the road. When Dad was home we went with him in the ute. He used to like sitting out the front of the pub to drink his lemon squashes in the shade and watch us. Or play pinball in the shop. It was sure faster getting to Bankside in those days. Doesn't it sound like a long time ago, November.

Flies suck my toe scabs. My thongs smack my heels. Saturday morning. Mum is still asleep, I'll bet. Never seen her sleep so late in my whole life.

'Mum hasn't been in to see Dad for a while,' I say to Tegwyn's bouncing plait.

She makes a wet sound. 'Because that bastard Bill Cherry won't take 'er in anymore. They had a blue on the way back last time. Couldn't you see that one coming a mile off. Pah! He's a greasy little bugger. Like to stick his nose in a mincer and then stuff it in his mouth.'

I just keep walking. She talks like that sometimes.

'Feels frigging guilty, that's why. Slimy little bit of cockroach snot.'

Gawd, she makes me guts roll sometimes. 'Fat reckons they fight. Mr and Mrs Cherry,' I say.

'Fight? Course they fight. Wouldn't you fight if you had to kiss cocky snot in your bed at night? Listen, Small Thing, there's things you just don't know.'

'And there's things I do,' I say, quiet, real quiet.

'Eh?'

'Nothin'.'

She stops and turns and I walk straight into those big hard lumps on the front of her. She laughs and pushes them together round me ears.

'What do you know, Small Thing?'

'Yer tits stink, that's what I know.'

'Up yer bum.'

'Won't fit.'

Next thing, I'm stuck in a blackboy with me legs in the air and spines up me shirt. By the time I crawl out, she's way ahead up the track, moons flashing white out of them shorts. She can still be funny, Tegwyn. It proves anyone can be funny, because she must be the saddest, angriest person in the whole world.

In a while we come to the place by the side of the road on a bend where all the dirt and bush is cut up with drag marks and a tree is broken off at the base. We just walk past it like we don't notice a thing.

Feels like a real long time getting into Bankside. We pass the big sign with its bullet-hole freckles, and the forest is way behind and the sun right on us. Mrs Mack waves from the shade of her verandah as we pass, and pretty soon we're coming up past the pub. There's always a strange buzz coming from that pub. It goes:

I-I-I-I-I! A man comes out to spit in the drain and look at the sky, and then he goes in again, pushing his hat hard down on his head.

Next to the pub is the drapers which Mr and Mrs Watkins run. It's got all balls of elastic and bits of material on rolls in the window. And a dummy with no head. And a little cardboard sign that says: *Gospel Meetings Sundays 11 a.m.* The drapers is always clean and unfriendly. Next to that is the shop. It's the post office, too, and also a couple of banks. There's a big verandah with an old sleepy dog and a pinball machine in the shade, and inside the flywire door there's the proper part of the shop – rows of cans and packets and bottles and boxes. Up the far end is the counter, a long shiny thing with the post office and banks on one side and the cash register at the other. Mr Firth is at the post office with his pencil in his black teeth and his hair all oily and sitting back. Mrs Firth is shaped like an icecream cone, fat at the top and skinny at the bottom. When it's hot, a map of the world comes up on her face. Africa goes right across her nose. She always seems to be smelling Africa and not liking it one bit.

Tegwyn and me sit out on the verandah for a bit. Malcolm Musworth is playing pinnies with the machine. He is back from boarding school in the city and his hair is short like his dad's. His dad owns the pub and a farm twelve miles out with its own manager.

'G'day,' I say.

'Hi, Tegwyn,' he says, without even looking up from the flashing silver ball.

'How's boarding school?' I ask.

He looks at Tegwyn's legs. 'Shithouse.'

'Doesn't he look like his old man?' Tegwyn says to me with a kind of pig-snort and goes inside. The bell tinkles on the door. Malcolm Musworth looks at me.

'Well, what about it, Ratface?'

I just stand there and can't say anything. I wonder if he's gonna belt me up. He's embarrassed.

'Piss off, Ort-the-Abort.'

I go for the door.

I get inside to the airconditioning where it's cooler and closer to Tegwyn. She's up the corner where the make-up is.

'Can I've a drink?' I ask.

She gives me a dollar from between those boobs of hers. 'Get me a Coke,' she says.

[33]

Mr and Mrs Firth watch us. They always watch you to make you nervous and clumsy. From the fridge I get a Coke for Tegwyn and a Weaver & Lock ginger beer for me. Mum says Weaver & Lock make the best ginger beer in the world.

For a while we stand around sipping our drinks, looking at things, just being cool in the airconditioning, listening to the clatter and ring of the pinny machine outside. The big freezers have got cold fog coming up out of them. I walk very slow past the rack of comic books. There is a sign: THIS IS NOT A LIBRARY. IF YOU WANT TO READ THEM, BUY THEM. I walk past so slow my knees shake.

Then I notice in the far corner of the shop, up near where Mrs Firth sits, a great pyramid of red cans. ARDMONA TOMATOES. The stack goes right to the ceiling.

'Wow,' I say.

'She's got the decorative touch, my wife,' Mr Firth says without moving his lips.

'Cor,' I say.

'Four hundred and twelve cans,' Mrs Firth says.

Right up to the ceiling. You couldn't put another can up. All red and shiny. The best thing I ever saw in this shop.

The door tinkles. I look around. A couple of yobbos come in. Black T-shirts, black beetle-crushers, hair all cut short. The kind of yobbos that drive loud cars with fat wheels. They kind of wade up the aisle with their boots going oink-oink on the floorboards. They see Tegwyn.

'Ooor,' one says. He grins and elbows his mate.

'Oooright,' the other says. They both laugh kind of dirty. My guts goes all tight and all that ginger beer fizzes in me and it kind of hurts.

'Can I help you two gentlemen?' Mrs Firth calls.

'Not as much, no,' one says. He's got a tooth missing. The hole is somewhere a mouse would go to live in. They both kind of wade over to near Tegwyn.

'Piss off, bumface,' Tegwyn hisses.

'Miss Flack,' Mrs Firth calls from the cash register, 'there won't be any language like that in our shop.' She gets out from behind the cash register and stands behind me, right near the pyramid of tins, like she doesn't trust me near it.

My guts hurts. I wish I could get out. The pinny machine

clatters away outside. The two yobbos just kind of hang around near Tegwyn like two fat blowflies until the one with the mousehole touches her shoulder with his finger and suddenly I let go a terrible fart and Mrs Firth makes a crook sound. Oh, that ginger beer! Weaver and flaming Lock! And there goes Mrs Firth swaying back with fingers pegging her nose. Tegwyn hisses like a cut snake. I look for somewhere to go.

'Get away!' Tegwyn yells.

'Listen here, love,' Mousehole says.

Oh, geez! The cans! Here they come and I'm running for the door. Tegwyn is running and laughing and the two yobbos just stand there and look like dags. The sound is like a volcano. Mrs Firth screeches. Running, running. We get to the door as the whole flaming lot comes down and one can comes out through the door with us and lands on the pinny machine and sets it ringing and the dog howling like mad and Malcolm Muswell is yelling: 'Free game! Free game!'

So. The walk back. We hardly got to Bankside and here we are going home. Still, it made Tegwyn laugh. She's walking just in front and it's hotter than it was on the way in.

'Wanna swim?' she asks all of a sudden. Even the sound of it is cool.

'Geez, yeah,' I say.

There is a deep swimming hole in the creek on the other side of the road from our place, just down from the bridge, and we head for it, sweating like pigs all the way. Every year there's the same deep spot in the creek where the bank shoulders out under a big redgum, where it's shady and thick with leaves under your feet, with an old rope hanging down that used to be for swinging from before it snapped and broke someone's neck. Now it hangs out of reach and looks kind of sad and funny.

After about a million years, we get to the bridge and go off down away from the house. The bush here is raggedy and only thick near the creek. There is even some green grass under that big redgum with the rope tassel. I take my shirt off and dive in and go right down to the bottom where it's all mucky and dark, and then I shoot up and come out yelling it's so good. It's cool but not cold.

The water doesn't move much. You can see the redgum reflected in it, and even that silly little bit of rope. I breaststroke around in circles.

Tegwyn takes off all her clothes and gets in slow, bit-by-bit. Toe ... ankle ... shin ... knee ... thigh ... waist ... and then she ducks under and a moment later I'm under too without expecting it. I kick her off and come up coughing.

'Just pullin' ya leg.'

'Yer justa kid,' I say, angry. 'No more grown-up than anyone else.'

'Ah, don't get snooty.' She spouts water and floats on her back.

After a while we go over to the bank and lie with our heads in the grass and the rest of us out in the water. Midges and dragonflies come and go. A crow calls from somewhere. Mostly it's real quiet.

'That was a good trick back there, boy,' she says. 'Saved by a fart.'

I can't say a word. I feel so important. I could go to sleep right here.

A bit later I ask: 'Are you happy?' But she doesn't say anything. Probably asleep.

When we get home, Mum has jobs for us. Jobs! On a Saturday! Tegwyn has to help hang out the washing. My job is different.

'What do you mean?' I ask.

'Go out and have a look at the chookhouse. Then you'll know what your job is,' Mum says, steam in her face.

I go out to the chookhouse and there is that lousy rooster with his neck sticking out of the wire. His neck is out, but there's no head on it. The only thing holding him up is his feathers in the wire. Oh, geez. Foxes. Or one fox, anyway. Must have just lay there waiting for that big dumb rooster to put his head out and ... whack, no head.

Out by the fence I dig a hole with Dad's shovel. The rooster is stiff and hard and smelly and stuck to the wire so that I have to kind of rip him off. Errol walks behind me as I take the rooster over to the hole. I wonder if Errol knows what I'm doing; he doesn't look all that bothered. Errol sleeps out on the dunny roof. I wonder if that's why foxes never get him. My brainy chook!

I know Mum'll ask me anyway, so I shovel out all the chook poop from under the roost and put it into bags for the vegie garden. Poop makes things grow – don't ask me why. It's one of those facts. All the hens go berserk as I shovel stuff out. The little chicks jump and squeak and look stupid. Chooks just eat and lay eggs and hatch babies and that's all. I wonder if they ever talk to each other.

I'm just tying off the bags in the shed when Fat comes over.

'G'day,' he says.

'Hi.'

'Playing with yer poop again?'

I shrug. 'Watcher been doin'?'

'Nothin'.'

Funny, you know, I feel a bit awky with Fat just now. Can't tell if he's looking me in the face because my eyes are on the ground, but I bet he isn't. The ground is all dried and cracked like Grammar's cheeks.

'Wanna muck around?'

'Okay,' I say.

I run up and tell Mum and she comes out onto the verandah with her arms all red and just looks at Fat, not real friendly.

'Be careful of snakes,' she says, looking right at me and then a long time at Fat. 'And mind how you walk.'

Fat and me walk slow through the forest, munching leaves and sticks and bones and dead grass under our feet. The air in you is hot as a baked dinner – you have to kind of chew it before it'll go down.

'You ever been to the beach?' Fat says.

'The ocean beach?' I scrape skin off my peeling nose. 'Nup.'

'A lot of people in the city go to the beach on a day like today. And all last week. Every day I can remember, they'd be down at the beach. Wish I had a surfboard.'

'You ever been to the beach?' I ask.

'Coupla times. If you get up in the morning and drive down there and through the city – and boy that's hot – you get there just in time to get wet and get home by dark.'

'You'd have to live in the city to go all the time.'

'I used to when I was a kid. I wouldn't mind living there again. I mean I wouldn't mind all that much. In the morning you wake up when it's real hot. You get up and go down to the beach. The sand is white and hot enough to make blisters on yer feet. It's really wide, a long way. Geez, the water is blue. Blue. And you have waves all around and lifesavers to look after you. Afterwards, you go up with your oldies to the beer garden and you get a lemon squash and sit in the shade and wait for the Fremantle Doctor.'

And now I know he's starting to bull me.

'What do you want a doctor for? Blisters?'

'What?'

'The doctor. You're bulling me 'bout a doctor.'

'The Fremantle Doctor, you dill. It's a wind that comes in the afternoon off the sea. Cool, it is. People open all their windows. You can see it coming; makes a dark line on the water. You can see it coming in from Rottnest Island.' He looks at me like I'm real stupid.

'I know about Rottnest Island,' I say, 'there's quokkas on it and Vlamingh discovered it.'

We come down to the creek, sweat all down us, and Fat is shaking something in his hand. Sounds like a baby's rattle. Matches. A box of Redheads.

'It's bushfire weather,' I say, kind of half-hearted.

'There's water close,' Fat says. He lights one up. I can smell it. Reminds me of lots of things I can't remember. He chucks it at me. I hit it into the creek.

'Don't be a donkey,' I say, a bit scared.

Fat lights another one.

'Don't be a stupid mongrel!' I yell as he flicks it at me. But it's dead before it reaches my hand. Fat looks all mean. His face is all bunched up.

'Don't, Fat. Don't! You'll make a bushfire!'

'Ya chicken, are ya?'

'No.'

'Reckon you are.'

What's he saying this for? What the hell's going on here? Fat has this ugly look. He looks like an angry porker going to the yards. I shouldn't have called him a mongrel or a donkey, I know it. But everything I say makes him worse.

'I reckon you should shut yer trap,' I say. It's like me mouth is angry and the rest of me doesn't know what the hell is going on.

Another match comes my way. I stamp on it.

'You Flacks,' he says with a hard laugh. 'You think ya hot shit. Butter wouldn't be yellow in ya mouth.'

'What's wrong with us?' My throat is real small, too small for words.

'Ya sister's a slut. Ya old man's a vegetable, and ya mum's a pisstank.'

And that's it. I'm going forward like some bit of a train that's busted loose and I'm rolling forward at him and he throws a match that I knock down hot at the ground and then I hit him and the matches go all over. His bum hits the ground. He kicks at me and one thong comes off. I kick him in the leg and then in the side and he's up like a ball, like a turtle, like a caterpillar, like a snail, crying, crying.

'Yer a fat slug!' I yell at him. 'I hate yer big flubbery guts and yer pig face and yer crybaby old man who thinks he's so funny and yer scrawny plucked-chook-piece-of-poop old lady. I hate yez!'

With a whoof! behind me, something else happens. I turn around. Flames. I turn back and there's Fat Cherry up and off into the forest heading home.

'Come back here, you . . . !' But there's no time.

The fire is as big as a forty-four gallon drum and running up the bank. I take my shirt off and wet it in the creek and run up behind the fire and hit it. The flames hurt my face and my arm and I hit them all, swinging around half-crazy and not knowing properly what the hell's going on. It crackles and spits. I'm hitting and hitting. I go for it like I'm attacking it, like I hate it to death. It goes on and on. Swing, hit, and then nothing, only black ground and smoke.

For a while, I dance around in the big, black patch, burning my feet, and then I fall in a shallow bit of the creek on my knees and just lie there.

A long time goes past before I move. I'm sore and hurt all over, like half of me has died. Bits of smoke still lift off the bank above. I roll over and look up at the sky between the trees, big branches like eyelashes across it.

[39]

The skin of the creek is black. Little things skip across it. I float downstream. I push off snags and rocks. I dogpaddle and breast-stroke down. You don't need an ocean beach or a Fremantle Doctor to know how to swim. Sometimes I pull myself along the bottom, it's so shallow.

I know when I pass the sawmill – there's our car roof still there on the bank. Down I go. I don't want to get out till I feel better. It's cool. The air is the only hot thing in me now. Even my brain has cooled down. Kookaburras gargle up in the jarrah. Stroke, stroke.

At the same log as before, I rest and peer across at the man under the bridge. There he is, still, on the bank in the shade with the bridge piles on either side of him. My hands hurt when I hold onto the log. I get back in under the water, crouched, and peer round the log. I look careful at him. How does he live? What does he eat? What's he doing so close to our place? Did he hear us this morning when we were swimming at the hole on the other side? I forgot about him.

Funny. I can see . . . his . . . I have to look real hard. I'm not far away. It's his thing, his old fella. It's real big and fat, up out of his pants like a periscope. And he's just sitting there in the cool looking at it. Looking at it!

Cor.

Reckon I better tell Mum about him. Real quiet, I swim back a bit, then get out and walk back barefoot.

We're all eating tea real quiet when there's a thump at the front door and shouting. Mum looks at me scared. No one's ever come to the front door before, except the Mr Wingham that came to tell us about Dad. Tegwyn sighs. It's steak for tea and I was halfway enjoying it.

'Tegwyn, will you go?' Mum says as Tegwyn gets up.

It's sad at tea with just the three of us. With two at the table it makes you feel real crummy.

'What's the meaning of it, eh? What's the meaning? Explain to me. Where's your mother?'

There's yelling coming from the front door. Mr Cherry, clear as day. He bursts into the kitchen, his singlet all wet and the black hairs on his shoulders all plastered down.

'Good evening, Bill,' Mum says. Sick-looking.

'Mrs Flack.'

'Well, what's all this?'

Tegwyn is behind Mr Cherry pulling dogfaces.

'I want your son disciplined,' he says.

'You smell of beer, Bill Cherry.'

'You're a one to talk.'

'You are in my house, Bill Cherry. I don't want to throw you out. You'll speak decently to me under my own roof, thank you.'

'And what's gonna stop me? Bully boy here?' he says, pointing to me. I stop chewing, gob full of steak.

'What's gonna stop you is me.'

'You're only a woman!' he laughs.

'It's a shame we can't say you're a man, Bill Cherry.'

He looks hit. 'What?'

'Any real man would've made arrangements for an employee of his who was maimed running personal errands. For a favour. Any real man would've owned up to it and took responsibility. A decent man would've offered compensation.'

'Bugger you, woman, I've driven you to hospital near on twenty times in my own time, on my own juice. Leaving me wife to run the place on her own. Bloody place is going to ruin –'

'Because my Sam's not there to keep it alive. Get down to the point of your rudeness, Mr Cherry.'

More banging on the front door. I go out to see. Mrs Cherry comes in like a runaway tractor.

'Oh, Mrs Cherry,' Mum says, back to the fridge, 'come in and join us. Your husband –'

'Come home, Bill Cherry.'

Tegwyn snorts. Mrs Cherry looks ready to kill. Tegwyn nicks off.

'Your children could do with some discipline, Mrs Flack. The whole lot of you could do with some gratitude, I reckon.' But she looks half-hearted about it.

'Your snivelling little son –' Mr Cherry starts.

'Now listen here,' Mum goes.

'No, you listen!'

'Bill Cherry.'

'Let go, Leila.'

'Get out.'

[41]

'Mrs Flack there's –'
'You'll get no bloody help from us when they pull –'
'Bill Cherry!'
'Out!'
'– him off the machines!'
Mum grabs a handful of mashed spud off the table and I get the hell out.

The forest moves quiet tonight. Jarrahs move a long way up and out of sight. Now and then I hear little animal noises. All these trees are dying, and all these little animals will have nowhere to live. One day the whole world will die and we'll die too. My back hurts and my bum stings and the backs of my legs too. I've got no clothes on out here in the forest. Prickles and burrs and twigs stick in me all over. I rub them in, squirm and shake around. It hurts a lot. I'm hurting myself. I want to hurt myself. I want to.

Over there I see the house lights. I dunno if they are still fighting in there. I hate all of this. None of this is fair. Somewhere I can hear a bell, a deep clonging bell, like the big bells in churches on the movies. Bong. Bong. Rings in my ears. Sometimes so loud it hurts.

I look up and see bits of the sky through the trees. None of this is fair. Not one thing.

I get sleepy. I grind on the prickles and burrs and sharp pieces of wood so it hurts me awake. It hurts.

Oh. No. Right before me eyes it comes up on its own. It's not fair. It's the last straw. It makes yer sick. There it is, me old fella with its nine black hairs, sticking up just like that old man's under the bridge. And here I am looking at it. Makes you sick.

There. I'm bawling. There. I can't stop bawling.

For a long time I cry until I feel sleepy and that bell comes back. I hear a car, close. The lights cut up high in the trees all around. The engine runs for a long time real close and I look over at the house to see it leaving the drive. Red tail lights leaving. Oh. I hope it isn't the cops. I hope there hasn't been a murder in there.

I get up.

There is something over the house. Like a cloud. *Like* a cloud. It glows, just sitting over the roof. Hell! It's bright as the moon. I start running towards the house, hit the wire fence like a truck and go flat to the ground and get up again all wonky and go like hell.

Mum is out on the back verandah, screaming her lips off. And I'm running. Feel my old fella flapping all over. Here I am in the nick, raw as a prawn, me shorts back in the bush, here I am running across the backyard.

'Moorr-toon!' Mum is yelling.

Oh. Not a murder. Please.

'Morton! Morton!'

She sees me coming. All of a sudden and out of nowhere, something hits me in the gob and I go down again. It's Errol. Jumped off the dunny roof at me. Me mouth's full of feathers and stink.

'It's your father,' Mum says, looking at me like she's not sure of anything in the world any more. 'Ort, he's awake. He's awake.'

I get up on one elbow, all embarrassed. Errol shakes himself, poops on my hand. Errol is a hen. A she. I never thought of it before.

II

Chapter Six

From up the road I can hear a car coming. It's a sound like a
waterfall from a long way off. Tyres make that water sound on the
road. I'm up on the big fat fencepost here, looking. A bunny
bounces out of the bush and onto the bitumen. Out the way,
bunny, you'll get chundered by the car that's bringing me Dad
home. Some ants crawl up my leg but I've got no time for them.
Have to hope they behave themselves. A long time I've been
waiting for today. Feels like I been waiting all my life, like I been
waiting since before dads were invented.

There. I see the sun off the windscreen and hear the engine
sound. Real quick, I pull the comb out of my shorts and push my
hair back off my face. Never wanted to comb me hair before in all
my life. Hear that engine – a big six. Dad likes a big six. Roomy, he
reckons. Give you room for your elbows under the bonnet. But a
terrible waste of juice, he always says.

Here he comes, slowing down now. But as they pull into the
gravel drive I can see another man driving, a man with short red
hair and a white jacket. I jump down and run beside the car for a
while, and before it leaves me behind up the track I get a look
inside and see my Dad lying in the back with the sheets and short
hair and a kind of nothing look on his face.

By the time I get to the house they already have him out on a stretcher thing and are carrying him inside and the bloke in white is talking.

'We'll have to see if you can manage. And of course there's no promises.'

'The doctor has explained it all to me,' Mum says, kind of flustered.

'And who's this athletic young man?' He looks at me. I don't like red hair.

'This is my son Morton.'

'Well, hullo, Morton.'

'Why isn't he walking?' I ask. 'Why wasn't he driving the car? What are you carrying him for?'

They stop walking with him and the sun hits us hard and the white sheet and the white suit make us all squint.

'I think we'd better get Mr Flack out of the sun.' They get walking again. Tegwyn opens the door looking squinty like she's just got out of bed, and I follow them in.

I didn't know this was going to happen. I thought he was going to be alright, but he looks pretty crook to me. From up the back of the house Grammar is calling.

'Is that you, Lil Pickering?'

'No, Mum, it's me. We've brought Sam home.'

Why didn't he bring himself home? What the hell's happening here?

'Shame about his hair,' Tegwyn says.

'Yes,' Mum says, 'he had beautiful hair. It'll grow back.'

'Took him years to grow it,' I say. 'He told me it took him years.'

'Well, he's got plenty of time to grow it back.'

'He looks like a punk with it all standing up like that,' Tegwyn says with a laugh.

'Short hair looks more manly, anyway,' says the man in white.

I pull a face at him when he looks away. I hate red hair. Short *and* red. Him and Mum go into the kitchen and talk quiet for a bit and I get a good look at my Dad. His face is pale and thin and it makes his whiskers stand out like pig-bristles. I pull the sheet down and what I see on his neck makes me yell.

'What's going on?' the redheaded man says, running in.

'Ort, what's wrong?'

'His neck! What they do to his neck?'

'It's a tracheotomy, son,' the man says. 'The doctors had to open his throat to let him breathe. He was all smashed up.'

Mum touches me on the arm but I don't look up from the big gob of sticky plaster that goes up and down with his breathing. A whistling comes out. Like the wind through the crack in a door. It makes me cold all over. Makes me bum tingle. A hole in his throat.

'Anyway, Mrs Flack, as I was saying, hospice workers will visit if you like and we'll rely on you to keep in touch. I'll bring the wheelchair in and show you how to set it up.'

While they go outside, I get a good look at Dad's face. One eye is all wonky and white at the edges. His mouth is alright and his teeth look okay. He looks at me with his one good eye and his one wonky eye as I open his lips with my finger. I can't tell if he knows me. I pull the sheet down further. All his chest is covered with sticky plaster. He has big white undies on that look like they come from the hospital. His legs are skinny and a bit yellow. There's all stitch marks on them and mercurochrome painted here and there.

Mum and the redhead come in with the wheelchair. Just the look of it makes me frightened. They hoist Dad up and slide him into the big armchair in the corner and prop him up with pillows, put a blanket on his knees, and Mum kisses him on the cheek.

Then the redhead goes, revving up his hospital's big six Holden. I sit there for a long time just looking at what's left of my Dad, listening to that cold draught whistling in and out of him.

'I'm not going back to school,' Tegwyn says, eating her tiny piece of steak. She starves herself something terrible.

Mum looks up. You can hear the whistling from in the lounge-room. Mum looks at her fork. 'Why not, love?'

'I wanna get a job.'

This kind of talk turns me guts. It's like a fight without blood or fists. Words going back and across. Makes you wanna keep your head down.

'You'll get a better job if you stay at school two more years, you know.'

'I don't wanna better job. Anyway, in two years there'll be no jobs.'

'Where will you work?' Mum says, looking real tired. 'There's almost no jobs now.'

'In the city.'

Mum sighs.

'You did,' Tegwyn says, kind of whining. 'You got a job early and that was in the city.'

Mum nods.

'Don't you like us?' I say. The words just come out of my mouth. I wasn't even thinking of them. It scares the pants offer me.

Tegwyn spits a bit of fat onto her plate. 'I hate it here.'

Then Mum is crying, hands over her face, elbows on the table, and Tegwyn goes to her room and I just sit there feeling useless.

'I thought Dad was going to be alright,' I murmur, after a long time.

'He will be,' Mum whispers, snuffling. Some snot shines on her lips and her eyes are angry with tears. 'He will be, Ort. I won't let him not be.'

Here I am up in the middle of the night, watching through the door cracks and the holes in the wall. There's an old sticker on Mum and Dad's door that says GET THEM OUT OF VIETNAM. There's a good hole right next to it. On the big bed, Mum is asleep with the sheet up to her ears, and Dad lies there with his eyes open, his toes moving a bit like they're dancing in the breeze that comes in the window. The house is quiet except for breathing in Tegwyn's room, snoring from Grammar's and that cold whistle from in there. He's still all busted up. He hasn't been fixed. He should be fixed.

It took me and Mum ages to put him to bed. Flamin' Tegwyn wouldn't come out of her room. We had to roll him and drag him like a feed sack, push him, pull him. There's his heel marks in the dust on the floorboards in the hall. How are we gonna keep it up? How? What do we do to get him fixed? He's not bad, you know. He's done nothing bad. My Dad kisses me goodnight and he puts his fingers in me hair and tells me stories and shows me how to do things that you don't normally think of. He sits out on the verandah at the back and plays his old guitar with the LIVE

[50]

SIMPLE sticker on it and teaches me chords that are too big for my fingers. He kisses Mum all the time and calls her 'Babe' like on the movies. He knows about trees and cars and chooks. He knows everything. He's flamin' better than everyone else's stupid dad, he can run faster and his hair is long like a Red Indian's. He never, ever, ever hits me. He loves us. He's good! Good! Crap! Turd! Shit! He's good, you hear me?

'Ort! Stop all that shouting. What are you doing out of bed? Get back to bed. You'll wake the dead.'

It shakes me up, you know. I thought I was only thinking. I reckon I'm going nuts. It's real embarrassing. But I don't go to bed. I can't sleep. It's lonely when you can't sleep.

This used to be a happy family. Everyone loves everyone. Why does it go like this? It's all stupid.

Outside, the ground is all bright like there's a full moon. I go out. There's no moon. The sky is clear and winking at me a thousand times. There's no moon. The light is coming from the roof. I walk out into the yard and look back at the house. There it is, that little cloud, small and fat like a woolly sheep, glowing bright. It looks like it's in exactly the right place there just above the roof. It's crazy, but inside me it feels like that shining cloud is the most normal thing in the world. And I bet no one else can see it. It just shines down at me and it makes me smile and I stand there until I feel tired enough to go inside to bed.

My porridge looks like fresh sick with all steam coming up out of it. I feel tired already. Dad is in his chair at the end of the table and Mum is giving him his porridge, feeding him like he's a baby. Makes me angry to see that. It took us so long to get him in there to the kitchen out of bed. Mum won't let him stay in bed. 'I'm not having him waste away in there,' she said. She won't use the wheelchair; it's still in the loungeroom. I'm with her on that. It's a horrible-looking thing. But it's so much work moving him. We can't keep it up. I know it.

'Eat your breakfast, Ort,' Mum says. She looks real tired.

'Can't.'

'You'll never grow up big and strong.' What does she think I am, a baby?

[51]

'Like Dad, I s'pose.' And straight away I wish I didn't say it. Mum's face goes all crook and white.

Tegwyn comes in with an empty plate.

'She ate it all. Like a pig.'

'Don't say that, love.'

'I'm sick of her. Why do I have to feed her? Why do I have to look after her?'

'You're older.'

'No, I'm a girl. Ort doesn't have to 'cause he's a boy, 'cause he's got a dangler and I haven't.'

I look at Mum. She looks surprised like she's never thought of it before.

'You and Dad always talk about boys and girls being equal. You're hypocrites. I'm leaving school.'

Mum still has that surprise on her face. 'Well,' she says, 'now we've got two people to look after. You'll have to look after one of 'em. I'll have to find some work to get us some money. Maybe Mrs Musworth'll give me some laundering. Now there's two people, an old woman and her son.'

'You don't think you're hypocrites, then?' Tegwyn puts her nose up in the air.

'I don't know.' She looks worried. 'Maybe we are.'

Tegwyn sits down to her porridge like she's not real happy with that answer. I keep my eyes away from hers. I didn't know she hated me for being a boy.

Mum sighs. The kitchen is warm. The fire I lit in the stove is going good. Lunch time, it will be too hot to sit in here. I look at Dad's eyes, try to see where they're looking. Wonder what he saw when he was in that coma. It's like his eyes are looking in and not out. Wish he could tell me about it.

And then there's a thump at the front door. We all look at each other.

'If that's Mr Cherry, you call me straight away,' Mum says, looking like one more thing will be the end.

I go through to the front door that we never used until lately, and I open it with a pull and there at the door is a big man with old clothes that you could buy at a school fete for fifty cents, a real long face with a big hoe chin, funny eyes, a book in his hands, and grass seeds all over him.

'Hello, Morton, is your mother there?'

I don't say a flamin' word. I know him. Me mouth must be way open but I can't help it. It's the joker from under the bridge.

In the end, Mum comes up behind me and says, 'Can I help you?'

'I'm not selling anything,' he says, then looks like he'd like to change that but can't, so he shuts his mouth.

He's big, tall. Wide hands. He could do with a wash.

'Yes?'

'I've come to help with Sam.'

Mum grabs my shoulder hard like she's trying to pop a boil out of it. 'Are you from the hospital, then?' Oh, look at him, Mum, does he look like he's from the flamin' hospital?

'No, I'm not from anywhere in particular. Nngth.'

I look up. What was that? He said this funny word at the end then.

'No, I'm here to help you bathe Sam. It must be time now.'

'I didn't ask anyone to come,' Mum says.

'No,' I say, 'we didn't ask anyone to come.'

'I understand that. Nngth.'

There he goes again.

'Are you from the Social Security?'

He shakes his head, smiling.

'Council?'

Mum looks at me. She wants to let him in, I can tell. She's mad. He's a stranger. He's dirty. We don't know who he is. We didn't ask him to come.

'We didn't know about any of this. Who's paying you?'

'I'm a voluntary worker.'

'For nothing?'

'Yes. More or less.'

She looks like she's decided to close the door on him, like she's suspicious after all, but then she just looks kind of scared and lost and she gives me a dry smile that says 'I'm sorry'.

'Well, you might as well come in, now you're here,' she says with a sigh. 'He'll be finished breakfast in a moment.'

We go inside to the kitchen where Tegwyn is feeding Dad his porridge like she's the angel of the house. Mum asks the bloke to sit down. He puts his black book down on the table and he's so big he makes the chair disappear.

'G'day, Sam,' he says to Dad. Dad swallows porridge and his eyes don't go anywhere special.

'This is Tegwyn,' Mum says, kind of nervous. Tegwyn just looks him up and down. 'And –'

'He knows, Mum,' I say.

Mum looks embarrassed. She's only got on the big tee-shirt of Dad's that she wears in the mornings before she gets dressed proper.

'I'll just go and get changed,' she says.

'No need. Really,' the man says. But she's gone.

Then the kitchen is quiet. I look at Tegwyn and Tegwyn looks at me. Now's the time I feed the chooks. I should be out there feeding the chooks. Mum comes back in with a pair of shorts on and a shirt.

'My name is Henry Warburton,' the man says.

'You've been sleeping under the bridge,' I whisper. He makes like he doesn't hear me. His eyes don't ever look at the same spot.

'Well,' Mum says.

'Come on, Sam,' Henry Warburton says, getting up. 'You could do with a bath, I'll bet.'

'He's not that dirty,' I say.

'I meant he might feel like one,' Henry Warburton says. He picks Dad up in his arms like he's a little kid, and asks, 'Where to?'

'You mean you don't even know the way to our bathroom?' Tegwyn says with a halfway grin. Henry Warburton smiles.

'Your Mum'll show me.'

Outside the bathroom door I listen. The water is running and it makes the walls hum. From Grammar's room comes the sound of Tegwyn playing the piano. She hasn't played in the morning for ages. Dad always wanted her to play it in the mornings. Grammar always did. She was the one what brought Dad up because his old man died when he was five. Grammar looked after him. She used to play the piano at dances in country halls all over the place. He used to sleep on the lid in a little fruit box. That's what he told me, or Grammar told me, I forget. Tegwyn is playing some old song that Grammar used to sing. Makes a lump in yer throat.

In there, in the bathroom, they're putting Dad in the water. No, they're testing it. The water's still running. Someone farts. Must be Dad. Henry Warburton goes 'Ahem'. I reckon they're embarrassed. Good old Dad.

Grunting, lifting noise. Putting him in the bath.

'Not often you see a man bathing another man,' Mum says. No sound from Henry Warburton. I can hear the water moving. Dad and me used to have baths together. In the winter when it was cold, I used to snuggle down into the hot and his big legs with all their black squiggles came up high out of the water. He used to sing songs like:

> You can get anything you want
> At Alice's restaurant

and he would hum and I would look at his old fella and wonder about it. You can hear the wind through the holes in the wall. Mum'd yell at us to get out, but Dad would keep singing and I would snuggle down in the water.

'Why are you here?' Mum asks Henry Warburton. 'Why are you doing this?'

'Does there have to be a reason? Nngth?'

'There has to be a reason for everything.'

'Yes.'

'Well?'

'I don't really know why I'm here.'

'I don't believe that.'

'Your husband is sick.'

'He'll get better.'

'Not on his own, he won't.'

'What are you saying?'

'I . . . Nngth. Nngth.'

I put my eye up to a hole and look. Why does he do that sound? Mum looks real worried. She watches Henry Warburton rubbing Dad's chest with a flannel. Dad looks like he's fair enjoying the bath.

'What are you?' Mum whispers.

'A man. A servant.' He runs his thumbs over Dad's wonky eyes. 'Only a man. Like Sam here.'

'What are you going to do?'

Henry Warburton looks at her and smiles kind of thoughtful, looks at her hands. 'I really don't know.'

Well that puts us all in together. Not one of us knows what the hell's going on.

'Lil Pickering? Is that you, Lil Pickering?'

Chapter Seven

He's out there digging in the vegetable garden. The sun is up over the trees but it's not too hot yet. The dirt he turns up is all dark and wet underneath. Mum's corn wobbles in the wind behind him. Cucumbers, zucchinis, tomatoes, lettuce, eggplant: it's like a picture, and he's out there in it, like something in the middle of a picture.

Mum comes out on the verandah with me. Her hair is all over.

'Is he staying, then?'

'Looks like it.'

'He's a bit weird.'

'Ort, you should hear 'em talk about us.'

'He sleeps under the bridge.' Mum says nothing. I look up and see her with her hair all crazy everywhere and her eyes squinty in the light, and I know she hasn't heard me.

At lunch in the loungeroom where it's cool, we're all eating salad as quiet as you can eat salad, and Henry Warburton says to me:

'Want me to teach you how to set a rabbit trap, Ort?' He has a big smile and a piece of lettuce on his chin.

'I orready know. My Dad taught me when I was six.'
'Oh.' He laughs. 'No teaching *you* any new tricks, then.'
I don't look up from my plate.
'Sam . . . is very good with him.'
'That's because he's my father.'
Everyone laughs and I dunno what's so funny.

All afternoon he works in the vegetable garden and the weeds pile up on the ground outside the wire that goes around it. The whole yard smells of fresh dirt. Reminds me of being little again when I used to eat it. He ties tomato plants up straight and pinches off little buds. In a box he puts long zucchinis and eggplants, a lettuce, some onions and a carrot. He doesn't sing or anything when he works. His back is white and wet in the sun. His daggy pants get real dirty. At the end of the afternoon I go and help him throw the weeds in to the chooks because I know Dad would be ashamed of me watching someone else work in the sun all day. When we are washing the vegetables under the tap at the tank, he looks up at my bat on the verandah.

'Wanna hit?' he says, pulling a face at the eggplant.
'Can you play french cricket?' I ask.
'I invented it.'
'Bull.'
'Well, I can play it, anyway.' He laughs.

We leave the vegies to dry on the back verandah and get the bat and the ball and start to play. He hits out of my reach. His big long chin digs into his chest and his funny eyes go everywhere so you don't know where the ball will go. He plays good and it makes me a bit mad and makes me feel okay. Then he hits an easy catch. I get it in one hand.

'You're not trying,' I say. 'You let me get that.'
'Yep.'
'That's not fair.'
'You shouldn't ever knock back a bit of help,' he says, pulling up his awful, dirty pants.
'I don't need it.'
'Everyone needs it,' he says. 'Sooner or later.'

I take the bat from him. He grabs my hand and it makes me look at his face. He's kind of smiling. He doesn't look so bad, really.

My hand is small next to his, but harder and darker.

'You're a good man, Ort,' he says. The ball is in his other hand. It's just the cork guts of an old ball. In his hand it looks like a fresh bird's egg, like it might break if he squeezed it.

'Why did you work in the garden?' I ask. 'No one asked you to.'

'It needed doing,' he says, holding my hand and the ball, looking from one to the other.

'What's that book you got inside?'

'A wise book.'

'What's it got in it?'

'Dreams, stories, poems, advice, jokes.'

'Nothing about cricket, I s'pose.'

He smiles at me like I'm really dumb.

'That was a joke,' I say. He lets go my hand.

'You *are* a good man. Wait'll they publish your gags. *The Portable Ort.*' Then he bowls quick, underarm and high on the bat and I kind of jump out the way and the ball nicks the edge of the bat and runs away on the hard dirt. He grabs it and lobs it across to me and I turn like a baseballer and hit it high. It goes up into the blue so you can hardly see it, but Henry Warburton is running across the yard with his big hands up and those dumb dirty pants flapping. He yodels as he runs and it kind of makes me laugh. His feet flop across the dirt. He runs backwards. The ball comes down. He leans back and gets it in one hand and then his feet go up above his head and he goes over the fence backwards with a yell, and comes down hard and laughing thin like a loonie. When I get to him I stop dead and look at the hole in his head where an eye was.

'It's orright,' he says, winded, 'it's glass. It's a false. Eye. Just come. Out with the fall.' I find it for him in the dirt. It looks like an ace marble, a tombola or something. He wipes it and puts it back in. It doesn't look so bad.

'How'd it happen?'

'When I was at school. Nngth. Was playing first slip. Ball hit me in the face. Crushed the eye.'

I help him get up. I feel sorry for him about the eye. Half his pants are still on the top barb of the fence. Mum is on the back verandah laughing.

I love it when we sit out here at night feeling the hot day go away and listen to the forest making its night noise. Sometimes when a car goes past out on the road, you get kind of surprised that there are other people in the world. Before his accident Dad used to sit out here with us and play sad songs on his guitar and tell stories. Like about the time Grammar had a fight with a man at a dance where she was playing piano and she knocked out his teeth with one hand and kept playing the bass part of 'On Moonlight Bay' with the other. He used to sleep in a box with *California Navels* written on it on top of the piano. He reckons that's why he always sleeps with music in his head. On nights like this Mum and Dad remember things and tell us. It's like the forest and the sky make them remember. Mum has stories, but she only lets them out in bits here and there.

'Be Christmas soon,' Tegwyn says. She files her nails.

Henry Warburton moves his bum to get comfortable. He's down against the verandah post. Dad is next to me on the lazyboy. Mum is in the cane chair. Tegwyn is in the hammock. It's dark, but I can see them all in the light from above the roof.

'What do you do for Christmas here?' Henry Warburton asks.

Mum sniffs. 'Oh, get a turkey. Go down to the creek for a swim. Muck around.'

'Get bored,' Tegwyn says.

'Not me,' I say.

'That's 'cause you're still a kid.'

'He's going to high school next year,' Henry Warburton says. 'He's half grown up.'

'He's too immature.'

Hope I am. Then I'll stay down and get out of high school. I don't want me head put down the dunny.

'You know what they call first years?' Tegwyn says. 'Melons. Yer gonna be a melon, Ort.'

'Least I'll be a watermelon,' I say, thinking of all those dunnies, 'you were a pigmelon, Tegwyn.'

'Cut it out, you two.'

Henry Warburton laughs and then he says that strange word, 'Nngth.'

'What's that word?' I say.

'It's nothing,' he says.

'Ort.' Everyone gets embarrassed.

'It's a thing I have,' he says. 'A speech impediment.'

'Oh.' Geez, he's got troubles, eh.

'Time for bed, Ort.'

'But it's holidays, it's early.'

'Well read, then,' she says. 'You can go too, Tegwyn.'

'Are you staying the night?' Tegwyn says to Henry Warburton. He doesn't say anything.

'Yes,' says Mum. 'He'll sleep in the loungeroom.'

Tegwyn sniffs. We go in. She slams her door. Me too.

I open my window. It's too hot to sleep yet. I can hear talk coming down in bits from the back verandah, and I wonder what they're saying out there where it's cool and good. So I do it. I climb out the window, crouch on the warm dirt for a minute, and then scrub along to the back of the house and sit in the dark at the corner. I can hear Errol scratching on the dunny roof. The light from that cloud makes the dirt in the backyard look mysterious, like the face of the moon.

'How long you been out here?' Henry Warburton asks my Mum. I can't see 'em because I'm just behind the corner of the house.

'Oh,' she says, 'sixteen years, more. Since just before I had Tegwyn. Sam and I came out from the city to try to get away from a lot of things. We were optimistic. Everyone was in those days. You know, there was Bob Dylan and the Beatles and everyone. We were hippies.' She keeps talking like she can't stop, like she hasn't done it for a long time. Which isn't true, 'cause we're here to talk to all the time. 'Sam and I met back in '67. There was a house in Subiaco where lots of people used to crash and come and go. Some got permanent. I'd chucked my job in; I'd been working as a secretary for a mining company. I just got fed up with being handled from behind.' She laughs. 'So I was living off savings. Running away from my father, too. He and me didn't get on. He was getting pretty rich from this fleet of hire cars he had. He thought he could treat Mum and me like we worked for him. Mum swallowed it, but I couldn't. She was used to it. Women of her age were used to it. Sorry, I keep getting sidetracked.'

'Keep talking.'

'Well anyway, I was living up the back of this house and Sam was living up the front. The house was full of muso types and people doing drugs. There was a guy who wrote poetry – what a prick. All of us used to sit around the fire in winter and just talk and talk like it was the most important thing in the world to be doing. People argued and cried all over each other. Sometimes it was fun. Other times it was just scary.

'You could tell there was something up between me and Sam 'cause I could never look at him and he could never play guitar in front of me. He was playing in a band called The Grasshoppers. This is gonna sound dumb . . . but one night when the talk got really intellectual and I couldn't understand it any more – I tell you, people who write poetry are such pricks –'

'I've written a bit myself,' Henry Warburton says.

'Oh.'

He just laughs.

'Well, it mightn't be true for everyone. Anyway, this night I got sick of it and went outside. I felt really thick, going out, like I was stupid or something, but I couldn't take it any more. And I bumped into Sam on the front verandah in the dark. He'd been out there longer than me. We were both really embarrassed, but I cracked a joke about poets and that made it easier. Well, that was all it took. That was the start of it all. We went walking, walked all night talking about things, telling stories about ourselves, bitching about the others in the house, till we found ourselves walking around Kings Park. That's a great place, you know, a big slab of bush right in the middle of the city. And there we were, walking around in this big bit of bush with all these trees around us and animals moving around, and Sam says, "You know, Alice Ann Benson, when we get married, we'll go and live amongst trees like these. People should always live near trees". And then we came out of the bush and there below us was the city with all the lights and cars and those big buildings and flashing signs. It was like looking over the whole world all of a sudden. We had a fight straight away. We argued for hours.

'But I married him. We hitched up here into the hills. I still had some money. We found this little place; it used to be a ranger's house before they opened the national park for felling. We've tacked rooms onto it over the years. We came up here and lived like hippies, growing our own vegies and milk, living near the trees – it was pretty romantic, you know. But it was hard to keep it up. I got pregnant and we got scared and Sam got work pumping petrol over the road. He had no trade or anything, but the

[62]

Parkinsons – the people who owned the roadhouse in those days – taught him how to be a mechanic. He still hasn't got his ticket, or anything. It was crazy, a hippie working on machines. He even got to like it. He likes fast cars. It . . . doesn't make any sense.'

'You okay?'

She's sniffing.

'I'll be alright.'

'He can hear us, you know.'

'How do *you* know what he can hear?' she says, real angry. 'Who are you to say? He's all busted up because of that greedy little pig Bill Cherry and fast cars and because he's a good man. Are *you* gunna fix him up? What right have you got?'

Then it's real quiet. After a long time, Warburton makes a hawk sound in his throat and says, 'She's got me there, Sam.'

For a while they sit there being real quiet and I push my toes into the dirt to feel it go cool. It's funny, you know, even though I'm immature and too young for my age, I feel older since Dad had his prang. I haven't tried to be, though I should've. It's just come on me and I didn't even know it. Well I think it has. How do you tell? These holidays better last. I don't want them to go quick. High school keeps coming up in my mind. I can see it at the corner of my eye sometimes when I'm thinking, and I keep it there. Geez, I don't want to grow up. Being immature is okay.

Mum sounds like she's finished her story. If I was her, I'd ask him for his. It's time he said something that makes sense.

Sad about Fat. I still like Fat. But I never see him now.

'So,' Mum says with a sniff. 'That's how we got here. Right now it looks like a nice dream turned bad. We weren't even real hippies. And now look at us – local yokels. We're more country than the country. But what about you? You're not giving much away.'

'Oh . . .'

'It's rude to let people spill their guts and then not do the same.'

'Have you done that?'

'Yes.'

'You don't talk much with people, do you?' he asks.

'Sam is all I need. He's all I put my trust in.'

I reckon Henry Warburton wants to keep us in the dark. From here you can hear Dad's whistling throat. It's not such a bad sound, kind of familiar and reassuring now. Reminds me that he's listening in, too. And they talk like we're both not here.

'Well,' Mum says, 'where and when were you born?'

'Geraldton, 1942.'

'You're older than us.'

'You sound surprised.'

'Living around Ort and Tegwyn, you feel like you're the oldest thing in the world. No, I'm not surprised. You don't wear it well.'

'Shame I can't slight you so gently in the same manner,' Warburton says. 'But for a woman living like you, working hard, away from cosmetics, roughing it, you've done well.'

'I wasn't meaning that,' Mum says, kind of cool with him. 'I meant you look tired and sick of things.'

'I am. But you're the one who should be tired and fed up.'

'I've got no reason to be. I live a good life.'

'And you guard it jealously, like your pride.'

'I don't like people speaking to me like that.'

'Well,' Warburton says, 'you've got a cheek. You just finished telling me how decrepit I look. A man has pride, too, you know.'

'Don't I know it,' she says. 'I live with two of them.'

'Geraldton must be the windiest town on this earth.'

'What?'

Talk, talk, talk!

'Geraldton,' he says. 'The trees grow at right angles to the ground. There's miles of sand dunes. Everything is clogged up with salt. A hell of a town.' He laughs. Across the fence and over the road, the lights are still on at Cherrys' roadhouse. AMPOL, the sign says, THE AUSTRALIAN COMPANY. You can see the lights on in the bowsers. The bowsers look like little robots waiting for something to happen.

'I went to Geraldton once,' Mum says, sounding a bit happier now. 'I had an uncle who was a crayfisherman. He got rich quick and lost the lot. Went to Indonesia.'

'Hell of a town.'

'What did your parents do?'

'Tried to stay married. My mother was a sculptress and my father was an Anglican priest.'

'Yeah?'

'Yes. And there was I in the middle,' Warburton says. 'I think they both tried hard to be what they thought they had to be. I don't know. They were in competition. My father was a very popular priest. People used to drive in from miles out to hear him.

[64]

Mum was successful too, in a small way. I was a believer, you know . . . well a kind of believer.'

There is quiet for a while.

'Why did you say that?' Mum says. I can hear her sandals scraping on the boards.

'Don't know. Think I'll go in. I'm really tired.'

'Oh.'

'I'll help you with Sam.'

As I scoot down the side of the house to my window, I see my shadow, fat and grey, running beside me. It's like running under a full moon. But, of course, there's no moon, only that crazy cloud up there.

Chapter Eight

My eyes open, and morning comes hot and white in the window. A dream is going out of me, out and away, leaving me awake and kind of sad. It was a crazy dream. I thought it was real, I really did. It was a crazy dream but it seemed right.

I was out at the edge of the forest just lying on my back, looking up at the moon. The moon was pale – it was daytime. Birds mucked about in the jarrah trees. It was nice there. I could smell the leaves on the ground. I could smell myself. Sometimes I can smell myself and it's okay. (It'd be awful to smell bad, like Malcolm Musworth.) As I was lying there with ants going past, feeling good because there were no jobs to do, I felt the ground go all funny, like it was shivering. The shivers went into my back. It made me feel cold and strange. I stayed there for a bit and it went away. A white bird flew past and went over the house. No one was around, not Mum or Tegwyn or anyone. Then it came again, the ground shivering like it was cold or frightened or finishing a leak, or something. Fences jangled around and twigs and leaves came down out the trees. I stood up. The house was kind of puffing and panting. I saw it from where I was – walls going in and out. So, I started running. I was thinking about Dad. I jumped the fence and Errol came flying at me and hit me in the chest and stayed there, and I stopped to look at the windows going up and down and the doors flapping. The ground shook. It made my legs all funny. I looked around for everyone else but there was no one. The sky went cloudy and dark. Then there was a crack like a tree splitting and falling and the back door came open and the house sucked me off me feet, sucked me in, and I flew in, feet-first into the dark house. Inside, everything was shaking. Like the house was taking off. I moved around falling everywhere, kicking things over. Plates and cups came out of the cupboards and smashed on the floor, the piano was going like a cut cat, playing something I never heard before, the TV was on its face, smashed, sliding across the room. That sofa with the crummy brown flowers was running around the loungeroom and I got the hell out. I could hear nails squealing out the floorboards. I lay in the hall. Suddenly, all the doors opened and closed and everything went dark and quiet. It took a while to get quiet, like it was winding down. Scraping noises went on for a while and something smashed and a nail hit the ceiling and then it was quiet except for little bits of plaster coming down on the boards. And then nothing. I was in the hall. All the doors were closed. It was dark. I was near pooping meself. I could hear me own heart whacking away. And then the lights started, blue, green, red, white, purple, blue, green, red, white . . . and it was like the inside of a fire. I couldn't tell where they were coming from, those colours. They got brighter and brighter till I could see all down the hallway to the back door, and then down the hallway came Dad. He was in the raw and asleep, and kind of sliding along the floor on his back, like he was being sucked along like I was, only slower. When he got to me, his feet touched mine and he stopped. That's when the lights slowed down, got fainter. I didn't know what the hell to do – I didn't know it was a dream – so I didn't do anything. The hole in Dad's neck was open and I heard him whistling. And then out of the cracks and holes in the walls and doors, all the holes I watch the family with, this white, thick light came, all going above us near the ceiling till it made a ball, a fat, mushy ball of white light. It stayed there for a bit and I just looked at it and felt like I wasn't frightened anymore and didn't care that I didn't know what the hell was going on. I watched as a little finger of light came out of the ball, getting longer, coming down to us. It pointed around – at one wall, the back door, the other wall, me, then Dad. And then it slid down to Dad and poked around for a bit and went in the hole in his throat. The ball of light got smaller and smaller as it kind of untangled and went into Dad and he started to shine white. He got so white I could hardly look. He was really white, like, like, like . . . really, really *white*, and I thought he was getting up, full of this light, but then I woke up . . . and here I am, kicking the sheet down, awake, and knowing already that today is gonna be a scorcher.

I lie here for a while. I can hear the chooks fussing. Someone is walking around. Someone is chopping wood. Listen – you can hear the split bits falling to the ground.

Two days Henry Warburton has been here now. Reckon I can't make up my mind about him, but. He's been fixing the place up and helping Mum and even playing with me and trying to teach Tegwyn some piano even though she doesn't listen. He's big, you know, and kind of ugly and got one eye and that thing that stops him talking completely right, but he's got a good laugh like a horse and he has a look sometimes that says maybe he could tell good stories. Long time since anyone told stories around here. Grammar is too old and in herself, and Mum is too worried and busy, and Dad can't talk any more. The only stories these days are the ones you listen in on, or the ones you figure out for yourself.

Yesterday, he walked into Bankside and came back riding an old yellow bike, a crappy old crate with a girl's carry basket on the front. In the carry basket was some clothes he said he scabbed from Mrs Musworth at the pub. They were old bits and pieces that men left behind in their rooms. Some had been there for years. They were awful and I reckon he didn't know.

His hands have got blisters on them. They are all soft and pink. What was he doing under that bridge?

'Do you think the bloke across the road would be likely to give me a bit of work every now and then?' Warburton asks Mum at breakfast. He eats toast with big, quick bites, like he's not sure if it's alive or dead.

We all look at Mum. She has a white shirt on, one of Dad's. It's too big for her but it makes her look young.

'No,' she says. She sips her tea.

'Not even a day here and there?'

'No. He keeps an eye on this place, you know.'

'What do you mean?'

'Him and Leila jump to conclusions. Anyway, they're both too damned guilty to give anyone the time of day just now. I think he's hit the grog a bit.'

'What do you think, Ort?'

I shrug. I dunno. I don't really get what they're talking about much.

'Why don't you and me go over after brekky?'

I nod. 'Okay.' Tegwyn is still in bed. Grammar is singing in her sleep.

Henry Warburton and me go through the fence and the bush clicks and ticks. There's a hot wind this morning. It makes the brown grass lie over and it makes the dead leaves fly and it brings the smell of the desert, or so Dad used to say. He said the easterly brings little pieces of the deserts and the goldfields and the wheat-belt: red dust and gold dust and yellow dust. The country is a nomad, he says, always going walkabout.

Cherrys' roadhouse doesn't get used much now. People go to Bankside for their juice because it's cheaper and there's a pub. Cherrys' gets people cut short or people who don't know about Bankside, or people at two o'clock in the morning when Bankside's shut. They used to sell lunches, too, but no one buys 'em. It's a sad place.

'What's he like, this Mr Cherry?' Henry Warburton asks. He puts his hand on my shoulder.

'Bit of a dag.'

'Ort, old son, you have the gifts of concinnity and concision.'

'Yeah?'

'Most definitely. Is that Mr Cherry over there? In the full blown flesh?'

Fat's dad is working on his front bowser with a screwdriver. His black pants hang off him until you can see the crack of his bum. He sees us coming, you can tell.

'Yep. That's him.'

We go across.

'Er. Mr Cherry?'

'You've found him. What.'

'I was interested to know whether you had any need of help.'

'Help?' Mr Cherry hasn't looked up from his bowser yet. Me and Henry Warburton just stand there and look down his hairy crack.

'Of the hired sort.'

'A job?'

Warburton looks at me and his eyebrows go up and up and up till they nearly drown in his hair. I almost laugh.

'I think you have my meaning.'

'I've got your number, too, smartarse. Piss off.'

Henry Warburton unzips his pants real loud. *Then* Mr Cherry turns around real quick.

'Oh, hello. You're with us, then?'

'Get off this driveway.' His face is all blue with not shaving and his eyes are red.

Warburton zips up. 'You have no jobs?'

'She's got a bloody hide sending you over here. She's got a hide, full-stop. Her old man still in the house, under the same roof.'

Henry Warburton moves real quick and has some of Mr Cherry's shirt in his hand and he looks very much bigger all of a sudden, but then he stops and lets go and stands back.

'I'm sorry,' Warburton says, 'that was silly.'

Mr Cherry looks frightened. I can see Mrs Cherry and Fat behind the flywire door and I feel all sick.

'What about my Dad's tools?' I say, without even expecting it. It happens all the time now.

'What tools?' Mr Cherry looks at me like he hates my guts.

'Some of my Dad's tools are still in there.' I point to the workshop.

'Rubbish. Anything in there is mine, you cheeky little bugger.'

'Come on, Ort,' Warburton says, taking my arm.

'You're a piece of poop, Mr Cherry!' I yell. 'My Dad is nearly dead because of you!' Henry Warburton yanks me away. We run across the road, jump the fence and then walk home. The ground is flat and hard and brown and hot. Grasshoppers hiccup all over the place.

'That wasn't a good thing to say,' Henry Warburton says. I don't say anything. I feel all tight and sick and hot. 'How do you know it was his fault?'

I don't say a word. Not one.

[71]

Later in the morning I stand outside the bathroom door and listen to Warburton washing Dad and talking to him.

'You can be washed in the blood, Sam,' he says.

I can hear Mum coming in from out the back, so I slip across into my room.

'. . . whiter than snow . . .'

I drag out the box of *Mad* comics from under the bed to see if they cheer me up. One says RONNIE REAGAN HANGS LOOSE. There is an old man on a horse. The horse and the man are smiling and have ropes around their necks. I dunno what it means. I wish it would make me laugh.

The hot white day swims along real slow like the sun is breast-stroking through that blue sky when it should be going freestyle. Everyone hangs around the shade of the house listening to the trees in the east wind. The ground is wobbly with heat. The house ticks. You can hear seeds popping, grass drying up and fainting flat. You can hear the snakes puffing.

Henry Warburton pokes around in the big shed all day. Hear him moving things, dropping them. Dad's Chev truck is out there. He bought it before I was born. It's older than any of us, except maybe Grammar. Every now and then Dad will go out there in the evening with some lamps and his tools. Me and Tegwyn and Mum sit out on the verandah waiting to hear the sound of the motor. But we've never heard it yet.

All day out there in the hot, Henry Warburton bangs around and we sit here inside wondering if we can even be bothered going down the creek; all day until the sun is gone and the east wind stops and we come out with Dad onto the back verandah.

But the same happens again: Tegwyn and me get sent to bed early so they can talk. Tegwyn slams her door and I slam mine; then she does it again, and so do I. I hear the springs going as she jumps on her bed. I knock on the wall.

'Piss off, Small Thing,' she says.

So I go out to listen again.

'Seemed there was more life in what my mother did. Out of clay or stone she made things that were alive. My father's conjurings with wafers and wine seemed more mechanical than her chipping away with chisels and bits of rock.'

'What was she like?' Mum is asking.

'Oh, I don't know, really. I never took the time to find out. She had long black hair she used to wind up in a bun, big red lips; she was thin. I suppose she could have been one of those Darlington wives whose husbands are bone marrow specialists with lots of money and near perfect accents. I don't know – I was so young. I left at seventeen. Went to university. I didn't even go back for holidays. I was supposed to be studying literature and music, but I don't know what I did all those years. It was fun, though. I wound up teaching. Lasted three months at a public high school. I knocked the headmaster over in the staffroom. I was in a hurry. He fell over onto the principal mistress and they ended up on the floor together. It was an accident, but I cracked a dumb joke about how she now qualified as the principal's mistress and that we should apostrophize her. I got the sack. They found some excuse and I didn't fight it. That was '65.

'Then I just started hitching around. Thought I was Jack Kerouac himself. It was really something to be young and not committed to anything except having a good time. I met lots of people, got into some interesting situations, did a lot of dope, experimented a bit. '67, I shagged out all of a sudden. Lived in a commune. North Queensland. I thought I was going to be there forever. I used to write poems and look after the kids. My book came out in '69.'

'What was it called?' Mum says. 'I've never met an author before.'

'I thought you lived with a poet.'

'Oh, he never had anything printed.'

'You'll laugh if I tell you.'

'It was a long time ago. I'll understand.'

Henry Warburton is quiet for a while. Dad whistles in the dark.

'It was called *Heavy Dream-Jazz from the Tropic of Capricorn –*'

'Oh, no,' Mum says, with a laugh.

[73]

'– and Other Verse Statements.'

'Oh. Oh, dear. Did you make all the poems look like flowers and motorbikes and things?'

He laughs. 'Yes.'

'Did anyone buy it?'

'Not that I know of. The publishers made papier mâché briefcases out of them, I think, and sold them to Chinese diplomats. I don't know, really.'

The night seems cool with their laughs.

'What made you stay at the commune?'

'Oh, a woman.'

'What was her name? Was she nice?'

'Her name was Bobo Sax.' His voice goes all funny. 'No, she wasn't nice. She had the voice of a man and she smelt like a labrador.'

Across the road Cherrys' lights go out. The roadhouse is closed early.

'Why did you stay with her?'

'Um. I couldn't not stay. I don't know. She was the exact opposite of my parents. She thought nothing, believed nothing, did nothing, pretended nothing. She wasn't nice or decent or restrained. I really couldn't say with any conviction that she was even human. She used to lie in her mud hut in the dark. The smell of her . . .'

'Yes?'

'Well, I stayed. 1970 I left. I don't know why. That was the year Jimi Hendrix died, wasn't it. It was as though I came out of a trance. I just dropped everything one day and walked off. I hitched back across the continent and went home to Geraldton. I got a shock. My mother and father didn't live there any more. It had been eight years since I left. The priest there told me my father was in Perth, and that he was a bishop. And my mother was dead. Brain tumour.

'I hitched back down to Perth as though I was stoned. I didn't know what I was doing. Someone showed me where my father lived. I found his office – it was fairly plush with lots of leather-bound books and dark furniture. My father was in. He didn't look surprised to see me. He poured me a drink. We stood there in his bishop's office with the sun coming in the high window, just looking at each other. He was wearing civvies – sensible cuts, sensible colours. His hair was grey and shiny. He probably couldn't believe the sight of me. I hadn't cut my hair for eight years. I didn't used to wash much then. I wore home-made clothes. He just looked at me and I just looked at him. Then he said, "Now neither of us has anyone on this earth" and then he showed me out.'

'God. What did you do?'

'Oh, I worked for a while, saved some money and went overseas. Easier to do then. Europe. I met a girl in Frankfurt. Married her and came back to Australia. In '73 our baby boy was born. We were living in Sydney. I had a job in advertising. Martha and I were happy enough. In 1974 she and the boy died in a rail accident. I drank myself stupid, got sacked, and went back up to northern Queensland.'

He talks like it's someone else doing all these things. So many things.

'To Bobo Sax?'

'Yes. I took a lot of acid and spent a lot of time with her. It nearly burnt me out completely. She died in 1977. It was a . . . bad affair. Our farm was burnt down afterwards by the locals. I ended up with nothing again.'

'That was seven years ago. What have you been doing all this time?'

'Oh,' he says, laughing, 'learning to live with nothing.'

I tell you, I don't know if I'm firing on all six. I just got this crazy idea and before I even decide about it, I'm up and off and doing it and the house is behind me as I cut across the firebreak toward Cherrys'. These days I just do things, like me parts don't need permission from me brain. It's real scary, like when I say things without giving me mouth the nod. Maybe it's growing up – or going whacko.

I move along real quick and quiet. The road is still warm when I cross it. The driveway of the roadhouse is oily and gucky under my feet. The big tin doors are down over the front of the workshop. AMPOL, THE AUSTRALIAN COMPANY. Round to the side window. Some nights I used to come here and watch my Dad's legs coming out from under a Chrysler or a Ford, listening to him sing and make noises with his spanners and I stood there for a long time knowing he couldn't see me, just watching his legs for no reason.

The window near the front is closed, but further down, the louvre windows are open a little bit, so I start working away at them. The first one comes out real easy, and I put it careful on the dirt and have a go at number two. Hard to see good. No moon. Stuck. I push and pull, try to work the glass out. Oh, geez! It breaks and comes away and I catch both pieces and feel the glass go in the skin and blood come up quick. I put the pieces on the dirt. The next louvre comes out easy, but with blood all over it. I scuff up on the ledge, get my head in the hole and kick in.

Suddenly there's lights and stars and rainbows and me head hurts like hell. The vise! I shuffle away from it with my hands on the bench, and then I get my feet in and I'm like a dog on the bench, sniffing around. I get down on the floor. Something chinks in the dark. Parts, tools. Up the front past the hoist I find the meterbox and try the lights. They all come on sudden and the place is so bright I cut them down to one little one low to the floor that gives everything a soft light. Radiator hose curls up near me feet. Boxes of old parts. An air filter. Fanbelts. Carbies. Tools, tools, tools, everywhere. Just tools. I can't tell whose they are. They all smell the same now; there's no telling one from the other. Some of these tools are my Dad's. He should have them back. But I can't tell which ones so I just stuff some into the old pillowslip on the bench that they use for a rag. Spanners, screwdrivers, things like that. On the way back to the window I see the Pirelli calendar from 1969 with the brown boobs pointing at me, so I grab it just before I decide to and stuff it in the pillowslip. There is a light green square on the wall where it was. I go back to the fuse box to turn out the lights.

The louvres go back in like they came out. They look alright except for the crack in the middle one and the blood all over. The tools chink and ring on the way back. All the way across the paddock and up the firebreak I watch the light above the house. It shows me where to walk.

'The first Christmas we were married, I wanted a Christmas tree,' Mum is saying as I sneak up the side of the house. 'Sam couldn't understand why, and anyway there was nothing like that around here then. That was before they tried re-foresting down near

Bankside with all that crappy pine. Christmas Eve I come into the lounge and there in the corner is a sunflower in a bucket of sand, decorated with old pieces of foil and bottle tops. Oh, I cried. I really love him, you know. People say they don't know what love is. Everyone says it now. They're scared to know. I'd suffer for him and be humiliated for him. I'd be ashamed for him and let people hate me for him. I have and still will. People don't want to know love. They might have to get dirty.'

Then she goes quiet, like she's said a whole lot more than she thought she would. I can hear Dad's slow awake whistle. Henry Warburton's shadow grows out across the dirt of the yard. He must be standing up at the edge of the verandah with the inside light behind him.

'Yes,' he says, just loud enough to hear. 'You're close to things, Alice. Close to all things.'

'And what does that mean?'

'Hmm? Oh, sorry. Nothing. I'm just waxing a bit lyrical tonight.'

'Oh.' She doesn't sound sure.

All of a sudden I'm real tired. This talk is way over. I climb back in real slow, pushing the curtains and the flywire away, holding the tools real tight so they don't chink.

Chapter Nine

Yesterday I saw Henry Warburton and Mr Cherry down at the fence. Their faces and hands were going like mad but I couldn't hear what they were saying. This morning I found Errol hanging off the clothesline with his neck wrung, and I'm not coming out all day.

Before lunch Henry Warburton carries Dad down the hallway to the bathroom in his arms. Dad looks so small, like he's my little brother now and my new dad's taking him to the bath. When we were small, Dad used to come in the night and take us to the toilet in case we forgot. He used to say to me: 'This is how I picked you up when you were still wet from Mummy's belly. So big now,' and I would still pretend to be asleep so he might talk more but all he would say was 'So big, so big now' as we went down the hallway with the wind going outside and the rain rattling hard on the roof.

I hear the water running and Henry Warburton's voice bouncing around in the bathroom. Later when the water stops, those crazy words come out, too big and weird to understand. Always those strange words.

A knock. Mum comes in with a tired face and her hair all down. Her face is so brown that when she looks tired or sad, white lines cut her cheeks up.

'Hi.'

'Hi,' I say, making room for her on the bed.

'Don't be angry. It doesn't help.'

'I know Mr Cherry did it.'

She puts her hand on my face. 'He drinks a lot, now, you know. He doesn't know what he's doing.'

I don't say anything.

'Henry's going over to speak to him later.'

'Tell him not to.'

'Why?' she asks.

'Don't let's even talk to them anymore.'

'Well, I'll talk to Henry,' she says. 'He's not feeling well this morning, anyway. Says he feels funny in the head.'

I push my pillow in two and lie back on it. Mum puts my feet in her lap and squeezes all my toes, one by one. Her green shirt has got patches on it.

'What does he talk about in there with Dad?'

'Henry? Oh, I don't know. I never noticed really.'

'He talks to him all the time.'

'I notice you don't any more.'

'I forget,' I say, looking at the wall with its cracks and holes. 'Sometimes I even forget he's here. Why isn't he normal now?'

She sighs. 'They don't know. You know what doctors are like. Talk a lot and say nothing. I reckon they don't know. And if they did they wouldn't bother telling us.'

'He doesn't look like a spaz or anything. He just looks like he's far inside like Grammar.'

'Sometimes he looks so sad.'

'Are you sure he'll get better?'

'He came back from the dead, didn't he?'

'Yeah.'

'Have some faith, then.'

'Faith?'

'Just don't give up on him.'

Lunch is quiet and I feed Dad his salad. His hands are going white; even under his nails it's white.

After lunch Tegwyn goes off into Bankside on the old crate Henry Warburton brought back. Mum sits in the lounge, mending clothes. Henry Warburton just sits with his eyes closed. I lie on the floor; it's cooler there.

'What was it like when you went to high school?' I ask him.

'Best years of my life,' he says without opening his eyes.

'Did you like it?'

'Hated it.'

'But you said –'

'Listen, leave it, will you?'

Mum raises her eyebrows at me. Henry Warburton sighs and gets up and goes outside.

'What's up with him?'

'I think he's crook, Ort. Don't bother him.'

'I just asked him a question.'

Mum shrugs. She pushes the needle into Tegwyn's jeans. I get up and go out. From the back verandah I see Henry Warburton going into the forest. All over the backyard, Errol's feathers muck around in the wind. Makes me angry again, and the dark patch that shows where he's – she's – buried makes it worse; I pass it on my way to the fence. Only a chook.

I follow Henry Warburton, keep behind him a long way so I can see him but he can't see me. His white shirt flashes in the red and brown trees. Birds scoot across. I walk careful over logs and dry sticks, make myself small to go through prickle bushes. I stop sometimes and look at him through a blackboy or around a tree trunk. He walks without thinking of snakes, and he doesn't mind making a noise. You'll never see any animals if you walk like that. In the bush you walk real wary, real slow. You put your feet down like you're not sure it's quicksand or not. You listen with your eyes and see with your ears. The same as when you walk through the house at night, keeping an eye on everyone.

We go down near the creek and pass the big black patch from the fire. He doesn't look. We go past the old sawmill. He doesn't look. Then I know. He's going to the bridge. But when he gets to the bridge he doesn't stop. He walks under and along the bank for a while till he comes to the swimming hole. I stop back quite a bit, high up the side of the slope, and get in between some blackboys.

[81]

Henry Warburton stops at the swimming hole. On the other side, the bit of green grass and the piece of rope look kind of funny and out of place. Henry Warburton sits down and takes off his shoes and socks. Then he takes all his clothes off and folds them and puts them over a log. Midges move over the water. Little helicopters. He walks into the water with his white back and bum showing. Then he slides under.

Flies get in me shorts while I'm watching and it nearly makes me giggle. Two of them going like a duck and drake, buzzing together all the way down me leg and into me shorts. I watch Henry Warburton float and swim and blow water. He gets out once on the grassy side, takes a run-up and chucks a bombie. He hits the water curled up like a baby. Water goes high up, almost to that tassel of rope in the big redgum. He comes up laughing. Makes me wanna get in too.

When he gets out he stands in the sun a bit. Then he picks up his clothes and walks back under the bridge. I follow him down and come closer because it looks like he's gonna stay for a bit. I breathe with my mouth wide open – it's quieter that way.

Under the bridge he just stands there in the raw, talking. Talking! To no one. His bum wobbles when he talks. Water still drips down his white back and arms.

'I hide and you see. I run and you follow.' I get squeamy; maybe he's having a go at me, like he knows I've been here all the time. 'To the ends of this earth, to the limits of the pit of myself, you will see and know me. Your love is terrible. Its gentleness a blow, its patience a judgement. Its silence thunders all about. Help me, Giver of All, I am unfaithful to men and to you, and even myself. Make my great weakness your strength. Oh, God, my Father and Mother, help me, let me love them, make me love them. I . . . I . . . carry . . . carry . . . you like a live coal in my chest . . . my . . . my . . .'

He's puffing like he's gonna cry or be sick and his bum cheeks go mad shaking and his legs all shivery. He holds his head with his hands.

'. . . my . . . God . . . save . . . take . . . wh . . . wh . . . whaa . . . ghh . . . nghh . . .'

He falls down and gurgles and his back goes like a bridge trying to come up through his belly. His hands dig in the dirt. All his muscles come up like polished bits of wood, popping out his skin.

He's hard all over like a piece of wood and sap comes out his mouth like he's turned into a tree.

'. . . nngth . . . nngth . . . ogh . . .'

While Mum is in the loungeroom watching Henry Warburton sleep on his mattress on the floor, I stash the pillowcase of tools and the Pirelli calendar under Dad's side of the bed. I look around, too, for Christmas presents, just in case, but there's none under there yet. Probably too early. I go back into the loungeroom. Henry Warburton is still asleep under the sheet.

'Get the mercurochrome, Ort.' Mum looks tired and dirty and her scratches are worse than mine. There's a cut under her eye, skin missing off her knees and elbows. I bring the little bottle from the bathroom and a clean rag from the bag in the linen cupboard. Mum puts the red stuff on me. It stings and makes the scratches look worse. When I put it on her it makes her look like she should be in bed herself. It was a long, long way back with Henry Warburton. I was already stuffed from running home and then back with Mum to the bridge. We could only carry him a little bit and then we had to rest. We dropped him sometimes. Mum fell over a stump and hacked her toes. I was crying 'cause I was frightened and sore. All stuff had gone dry on his face. He looked dead.

'Now we've got another one to look after,' I say.

'Don't get it in my eye,' Mum says. She tries to show how much it doesn't sting.

Tegwyn comes in, sweaty and red from riding. 'What's up?'

'Henry chucked a mental,' I say, 'down by the bridge.'

'It was a fit.'

'Is he an apoplexic or whateveritis?'

'An epileptic, Tegwyn,' Mum says. 'I don't know.'

'Lucky he wasn't swimming,' Tegwyn says, putting her bag on the sofa.

'He was in the nick,' I say, with a grin that won't go away.

Dad sniffs; it makes us all look around, but there's no kind of look on his face that's special.

'Beaudy,' says Tegwyn. 'Now there's three.'

She goes down the hallway again and soon we hear music from the piano. It's kind of nice: up and down sounds, up and down.

'That's Grammar's music,' Mum says, just sitting there. 'She used to play it all the time when she first came here. It's the kind of music they never let her play at the socials and in the dance halls.'

'It's nicer than plonky-plunk music.'

'Yeah. It's German.'

'How long's Grammar been here?'

'Since the day after you were born.'

'I don't get some things.'

'Understand, you mean?'

'Yeah.'

'What don't you understand?'

'Why Dad's crook. Why Grammar is so old and inside herself. Why *he*'s here, and why he baths Dad and talks funny and chucks a wobbly in the bush so we have another one to look after.'

'Is that all?' Mum says with a laugh.

'Why Tegwyn doesn't like us. Why Mr Cherry is ... Mr Cherry ...'

'You've got me there, mate. I don't know either. Crazy, isn't it?' She's got wet eyes. 'Bloody crazy.'

Henry Warburton wakes up and doesn't know who the hell we are. He walks around real soft. He doesn't remember. He's all arse-about. Doesn't know his own name. He starts laughing and then bawls his face out into Mum's Sydney Harbour Bridge teatowel. We put him back to bed and he sleeps and sleeps until morning.

Just as the sun is up I find ten chicks under the chook I call Bruiser. She pecks me away but I get a look and count 'em real quick. I go to the shed and get them some mash. Bruiser gets off for a while and I grab a little pecker and take him inside.

'There's chicks,' I say at the kitchen table. I open my hands.

'New life,' Henry Warburton says. He looks at the chick like it's hard to see. He goes on eating.

'That means there's chook for dinner tonight,' Mum says with a smile.

'Why?' asks Henry Warburton.

'Because we always do,' I say.

Mum shrugs. 'A kind of celebration, I s'pose. Will you do it for us?'

'What?'

'The chook.'

'*That?* Kill it?'

'No.' She laughs. 'A big one, silly.'

'No.'

'You eat chicken, don't you?'

He nods. 'I won't kill.'

'Sam always says everyone who eats vegetables should grow their own at least once, and everyone who eats meat should kill it at least once, so they know what it means to be responsible. And so they remember who and what they are and why they keep living.'

Henry Warburton gets up and goes into the loungeroom. Mum looks at me, and I know what it means. Me guts goes funny.

After breakfast I put the chick back and catch a fat young hen. I tie her up like Dad does and hang her upside down from the clothesline so she goes calm. I bring the machete from the shed, take the chook down the back and take her head off on the block. I don't let her go. Dad says it's an abomi-nation to let an animal run round without its head. Mum brings the hot water out. The feathers come off easy. It stinks. I pull the guts out, wash it, and it's all over. Henry Warburton can go hungry tonight for all I care.

For two days he walks round like he can't remember what he's doing in our house. He shouts things in his sleep like: 'They have given the dead bodies of your servants as food to the birds of the air, and the flesh of your saints to the beasts of the earth!' He cries in his sleep. Mum washes his sheets every morning because of the sweat, and then one morning when we're looking at the little chicks running around on their own, yellow and brown, he comes out in his pyjamas and says, 'I'm better now'.

Mum and Tegwyn and me just look at him. The pyjamas are too small; the leg ends are nearly up to his knees. Tegwyn says to him, 'Are you sure?' and we all laugh because he looks such a dag and the chooks stare at us like we're dumb animals and don't know any better.

[85]

Chapter Ten

And then out on the verandah in the warm dark he blurts it out.
We're all quiet, just sitting listening to the night in the forest and
the chooks sleeping and Dad whistling in-out, and Warburton
starts talking like it hurts him but he won't stop. I look at the stars
and try to see what they're saying with those bright little mouths
going open and closed all the time. The sky goes way back
tonight; it's like looking into water, and you wonder why you
can't see your reflection at the bottom, but you know you can see
something. Henry Warburton makes us all jump with his quick
words.

'It's time I stated my purpose. I haven't meant to be deceitful;
God has sent me here.'

Dead quiet. At the end of the dead quiet Mum says, 'What do
you mean?'

'So very hard to explain. I know you won't believe me, but I had
a vision.'

'What's that?' I ask.

'It's something you see that no one else sees. It's real, it's there,
but only you see it.'

'Like the light,' I say.

'What light?' Mum says.

'The one up the roof. It's a cloud kind of thing. Look, it lights up the yard. You can see rabbits' eyes in it all round the fence.'

'Don't talk crap,' Tegwyn says. 'There's no light, there's no rabbit eyes. It's pitch black out there. If your brain worked as well as your imagination you wouldn't be so thick.'

'Tegwyn,' Mum says, 'leave off.'

'Well, what did *you* see?' Tegwyn says to Henry Warburton.

'It's not important. I just saw.'

'Oh, bollocks.'

'Tegwyn, another word like that and you can go to your room. Don't be so damned rude. Go on, Henry.'

'God told me to come to you.'

'Who's God?'

'Ort, be quiet.'

'No, it's alright,' Henry Warburton says, sounding like it really does hurt to talk like this. 'God is who made us and made the birds and trees and everything. He keeps things going. He sees all things. He is our father. He loves us.'

'I thought it was just a word. Like heck. Is he *someone*? Mum?'

'I never really thought about it, Ort . . . I, I –'

'So what did he send you here for?' I ask Henry Warburton.

'To love you.'

Tegwyn groans. 'I thought you said you were alright.'

'Did you get our names from God?' I ask him. 'How did you know our names? You knew all our names, and you knew about Dad.'

'He was living down at the bridge spying on us. He watched us swimming –'

'But –' I start.

'And I had no clothes on. Did God tell you what me fanny looks like, too?'

Mum stands up, skraking the cane chair. 'Tegwyn, go to your room.'

Tegwyn slaps the back door against the wall. The flywire pops out the frame. We hear her door slam. After a bit, Henry Warburton keeps talking and we listen. He talks and talks about this bloke Adam and this bloke Eve who had no clothes on and it didn't matter 'cause they ate fruit and talked to a snake and it was a bad thing, and everything went wrong-oh. And how you can see God but you can't. And all these stories about God in burning bushes and piles of fire and tornadoes and little clouds. Stories! Piles of 'em. He tells stories like you've never *heard*, boy. About God getting sad when no-one loved him, and him just waiting around keeping things going, waiting for someone to like him, and then getting angry and crying and making a flood with his tears. This bloke Noah and his boat. I know that story from school. Another one about a kid fighting a monster, and this one about a bloke trying to run away from God and how he got swallowed up by a big fish and chundered up again. I saw that on telly. All the time he's talking about this bad in people and God wanting people to love him but they can't because of all this black bad in them like in an apple. And this real long story about God making a kid in a girl's belly. This kid grows up and some like him and some don't. He can do crazy things like walk on water and then make it into plonk, make crook people better and dead people alive. People didn't like him because he was so good to them. They killed him by sticking him on a tree. They put him in a hole but he got up afterwards and went up into the sky with God.

At the end of the story it's real late, but I feel like I just got out of bed. My head's ticking away and me hands are all tingly. All the red eyes of the rabbits out near the fence are dancing. Mum sighs.

'So. You're a preacher.'

'Yes. An evangelist, I suppose you'd say.'

'Well why wait until now to start preaching?'

'I've been preaching since the moment I arrived. I'm sorry, I don't do it well.'

Mum sniffs; she does when she's thinking.

'So, God's up there?' I say, pointing to all those wonderful stars. 'A someone?'

'Everywhere, Ort. He's in everything. The trees, the ground, the water. Everything stinks of God, reeks of him.'

'But he's up there a lot?'

'Well, they call him the Father of Lights.'

'He sees *everything*?'

Henry Warburton sighs, and then again. 'Yes, Ort, every little thing.'

'Then he knows the secrets.'

'What secrets?' Mum says; she sits up straight.

'All the secrets. All our secrets.'

'Yes,' he says.

[89]

'And he saw who killed Errol.'

'Ort.'

'And what happened to Dad. What he's thinking. And he knows what Grammar's always thinking.'

'All . . . all the mysteries. All secrets.'

Sounds right to me.

Mum sniffs. Henry Warburton laughs. Out over the forest, a star tumbles out of the black eye into the trees. Tomorrow I'll go and look for it.

'Did you make a wish, Ort?' Mum says.

'Yes.' Not true. I forgot.

For a while it's quiet, like everyone's thinking. There's lots of questions in me, and this feeling right down that makes me feel like I'm jumping in the air, or like when you hit a bump going real fast in a car. Butterflies, bellyrolls.

'You never mentioned any of this before,' Mum says to Henry Warburton. 'When you talked about yourself. Not a word. Why did you do that?'

'Because,' he says, real quiet, 'because . . . I'm weak.'

'Yes, I can see that now.'

'You don't like weak men.'

'No,' she says, 'all men are weak. A woman's got no time to be weak. It's not that I don't like weak men. I just get sick of them. Bill Cherry, for instance. He takes out his weakness on children.'

'And Sam?'

'I count Sam with the children.'

'I don't understand.'

Mum sniffs. 'Sam is a child in a man's body. He trusts people. He thinks the best of them. He sees the way things should be, not always the way things are.'

'And he can hear every word, Mum,' I say, grabbing hold of his hand. 'You forget.'

She looks at me. I can see the water in her eyes in the light from the roof. Her hands are all tight and twisted together the way two brown, fighting spiders would be. She nods, real slow.

'Even kids've got ears,' I say.

'Sometimes their ears are too big for them and they hear too much,' Warburton says, like he's not in a good mood.

'Not as much as some,' I say, pointing up there into the night.

[90]

Henry Warburton gets up and for a sec I don't know what he's gonna do, but he just steps off the verandah onto the dirt and walks out into the middle of the yard with his hands in his pockets, kicking with his feet, whistling some tune or other. He stops and turns around, looking up, looking round with all that black and white winking behind him.

'Afraid I can't see your light anywhere, Ort.'

'It's there,' I say.

'I can't see it.'

'I can't see what you see, either.'

'I'd say you've got a match, here, Henry,' Mum says, laughing like she feels better all of a sudden.

I squeeze Dad's hand, worm me fingers between his and squeeze. There's no squeeze back, but that doesn't make me feel different.

'Anyone for a cuppa?'

We all say yes except Dad who never says no to a cuppa. We go in when the kettle's boiled, and bring out the pot and the cups and a tin of Mum's bickies – the ones made of bran and oatmeal that go through you like the charge of the life brigade. We sip and dunk and I help Dad. It's not that his hands and mouth and eyes don't work; it's just like he's not interested in using them any more. It's like he's given up. We eat and drink and go quiet again; the tea and bickies makes us friendly.

Mum makes herself a second cup, and me too; makes you feel real grown-up, two cups. She looks like she's gonna say something for a sec, and then she looks at Henry Warburton and then at her cup of tea and says nothing. He smiles.

'I was converted, if that's what you were going to ask.' Mum smiles and looks kind of embarrassed. 'God is a mystery. He plants his love in the path of all our plans.'

'Aren't you tired, Ort?' Mum says.

'No, is this secret?'

'Of course not,' Henry Warburton says. 'Of course not. What was I saying? Oh, our plans. I had a lot of plans after Bobo died. Plans to get a job. To go away again. To buy a farm. To kill myself. One morning I woke up with this awful haze in my eyes. It was like looking into a sixty-watt bulb. I had it for three days before I went to the first doctor. This terrible light in front of my eyes. It hurt. I had headaches, I couldn't see properly. I couldn't continue a normal life, couldn't keep a job. I went to doctors, eye specialists, even a psychiatrist. None of them could help, though they all had different explanations for the same phenomenon. It went on and on. I was staying in this boarding house in Brisbane. The landlady was a crazy old thing with a hearing aid like 1950's TV – almost big enough to have to strap it to her back. She used to climb the stairs day and night, shouting: 'In my father's house are many rooms!' I just thought she was a nut. I ended up completely immobile in my room with this shocking light and pain and this feeling of not quite being attached to myself, and she came in, morning, noon, and night, nursing me and cashing my dole money for herself. I got worse. I fought it, thought I was going blind, so I fought against it, and it was like a cramp when you're swimming – the more you fight it, the worse it gets, the quicker you drown. It brought on nightmares and I must have been out of my mind in the end, fighting it, fighting it, all the time this white light burning into me. I don't recall much of it. It was a week or so of it. I think I just gave up, something inside of me just broke and surrendered. I was utterly exhausted and it went away. I looked around for a moment, at the cobwebs in the corner of the ceiling, the brownish curtains, and I just fell asleep. Woke up two days later and there was the landlady – Mrs Sims was her name – with a bowl of soup, ready to feed me. She didn't smile. She just said, "God has been with you" and stuffed an iron spoonful of her awful soup in my mouth.

'Recuperating was almost as bad as going through the experience itself. I was constipated to the point of no return. Concrete laced with razor blades.

'When I got better, I went out and stole a Bible from a shop that sold heavy Catholic theology and plastic Marys. I started travelling again. Met farmers, wanderers, bush philosophers who were believers. Blokes in road gangs. Barmaids. And I realized that the Church did exist. The kingdom without walls. Family of Man, or whatever. It was a terrible shock after being brought up by a High Church agnostic. I learnt a lot of things. Lived in a community in Gippsland for a year. There we were, God was with us and in us, without us having to say the secret formula. We didn't need to conjure God up with wafers and wine. He's always been there only we never look. All you need to do is open your eyes. You see, and then you either want it or you don't. If you believe, the Spirit helps you to believe more. Helps you to love more.'

[92]

'But you had to have them opened.'

'Sometimes we need a bit of prompting.'

'And now you're out here prompting the Flacks,' Mum says smiling over her cup. I suck on tea leaves.

'Yes, here I am. Proselytizing the heathen Flack.'

'You could actually say you've seen the light,' Mum says, with a laugh.

'I suppose so.'

'I can't figure you out,' she says, shaking her head.

He laughs. 'You know what my middle name is? Esau. I think it was a joke my father thought I'd appreciate when I was old enough to understand. He used to call me Esau the see-saw. Up and down. Yes and no. Good and bad. The blind leading the blind.' Again, he laughs. 'Esau selling his birthright for a pot of lentil stew. Literally. We ate a lot of lentils in northern Queensland.'

'They're good for you,' I say.

'Yes,' he says grinning, 'but they make you fart something awful.'

'Everything has a price,' Mum says. We all laugh. The chooks shuffle on their perches and the rabbits move red eyes in the dark.

Chapter Eleven

It's real early in the morning. The creek is flat brown and the swimming hole looks like someone just painted it for us, like God just did it. Down here at the bridge it's real quiet. Mum, Henry and me are standing in the water, and Henry is talking. Everything's stopped except us.

'Do you believe, Alice?'

Mum looks at me. 'Yeah. I reckon.'

'Then I baptise you in the name of Father, Son and Spirit.' And under she goes, with Henry holding her. When she comes up, her dress sticks and her hair is flat. She splutters and laughs a bit.

I stand there, nervous. Think about what Henry told us that night a couple of days back. Yep, it still sounds right. He turns to me. I feel the mud in my toes. I see a bird frozen still in a tree behind Henry, and up by the bridge, Tegwyn hiding to watch. I feel sad a bit.

'What about you, Ort?'

'Yeah. I believe it.'

He crosses my hands on my chest and holds me big and strong and I go back like I'm falling out a window, out into the sky forever, and I keep my eyes open under the water and it's like tea and it all goes up me nose and then I'm rushing up to the surface like out of a dream. And there's the sky. All over. And it all starts again. That bird calls out and chops off somewhere, and it's quiet under the sky. And I laugh a bit too.

Chapter Twelve

This morning when all the birds were starting to make their heep-beeb waking-up sounds, Henry Warburton rode off on the old yellow bike. He had a white shirt on and black pants, and shoes. He rode down towards Bankside. I saw him go, and I don't think he saw me. A couple of weeks, he's been here now. Things are different. The sky was all pink. Everything was still. I knew then it would be a cooler day; could smell it in the ground. Mum was up and getting breakfast when I went in. I told her Henry was gone and she looked like she was worried but trying hard not to look like it.

'What about the Lord's Supper and the praying and the Bible story?' I said.

'Oh,' she sighed and put more wood in the stove. 'I s'pose we can do it ourselves. That's what Henry said. Don't need anyone to do it for us.'

I was a bit nervous, but we did it. We sat down at the table while the eggs were on and the bacon, and I read.

In this you greatly rejoice, though now for a little while you may have to suffer grief in all kinds of trials. These have come so that your faith – of greater worth than gold, which perishes even though refined by fire – may be proved genuine and may result in praise, glory and honour when Jesus Christ is revealed. Though you have not seen him, you love him, and even though you do not see him now, you believe in him and are filled with an inexpressible and glorious joy, for you are receiving the goal of your faith, the salvation of your souls.

The bloke who wrote that once cut off someone's ear. You'd think that someone who went round cutting off people's ears could tell a better story. Anyway, the eggs and bacon were ready by then, so I stopped and Mum said a prayer.

'Thank you Jesus for this good food please make us good and Sam better Amen.'

And then we ate breakfast. At the end of breakfast we did the Lord's Supper like Henry Warburton's been doing with us since we got baptized last week. Mum got the sherry and some bread. Then she said the words she could remember.

'Take it, it's my body.' She gave me some bread and took some herself. We ate it. 'Drink all of it,' she said, pouring some sherry in my tea mug. There were tea leaves floating. 'It's for forgiving sins.'

Then I said: 'We love you God Amen.'

That was this morning. We did it all again at lunch 'cause it's as often as we meet, like it says. It's not really the blood of Jesus. Any dumbo can see that. Henry says it's just to remember. It's no use eating Jesus. Ha! He's in you already.

And now I'm here wiping up for Mum. Christmas is five days away. Maybe Henry Warburton's gone off to buy us prezzies, eh. I can hear the forest sighing like it sleeps in the day and wakes up at night. Mum scrubs away at a pot, her arms all red.

'How big's a soul, you reckon?' I ask. She blows a bit of hair out her eye.

'Oh, I don't know,' she says. 'Big as your fist.'

'He fits in small places.'

'Who?'

'God.'

'Well, he's a mystery,' she says. 'That's what Henry reckons.'

Getting baptized was real weird, but kind of fun. Henry asked if we were into it, if we believed all the stories and stuff, and I said yes real quick, specially after him talking about being born twice and coming back from the dead. I know about that stuff. So does Dad. We've both come out of comas, and I was dead twice. I had to learn to walk and talk again. Dad will too, if he ever gets better. So, I was into it. Mum said yes in the end. She said she didn't know. He explained it all again. Took ages. In the end she said yes. Tegwyn said it was a load of crap and ran out the room. Henry Warburton shrugged and looked sad.

And now we're Christians. Things change fast round here. Henry Warburton turning up out of the blue like that, giving us all this stuff about Jesus, me going to high school next year, busting up with my best mate Fat Cherry. And Christmas real soon. Feels like I'm growing up. You can't be immature for ever.

We finish up the dishes and then go in and get Dad out of his bed for a bath. With Henry Warburton away, it's gonna be real hard looking after Dad again. He's hard to move; he falls all over like a bag of chook poop. Mum and me get him on the floor and drag him. The wheelchair is in the corner, but Mum won't have a bar of it.

'Berrrrgfh!' Dad burps.

'Beaudy, Dad.'

'Morton,' Mum says, 'pull your weight.'

We drag him down the hall and leave tramlines in the dust with his heels. The water is going already – thunder in the bathroom.

'Is that you, Lil Pickering?' Grammar calls out.

'No, it's just us, Grammar!' I yell.

We get Dad out of his PJ's and in the water. His head goes under. Mum pulls him up by the hair.

'Yer swimmin', Dad,' I say.

'Sorry, love,' Mum says.

We get out the flannels. Dad's chest hair goes like grass in the wind.

'You think he knows about his soul?' I ask.

'He used to always talk about his heart speaking to him,' Mum says. We always say 'used to', like he's in the past now.

'He must know about God,' I say, soaping his face. He looks at me with those inside-of-himself eyes. 'He's into trees and animals. And *you* reckon he's like a kid. Henry says we're s'posed to be like kids. It's easier for kids to be like kids, though, isn't it?'

'You talk too much.'

'You mean I hear too much.'

[99]

She chucks a flannel. It hits me in the gob. I chuck it back. Then it's on, me and Mum mucking around like kids, chucking water and sending it all over the asbestos walls and flying in Dad's face.

Then I get an idea. I stop flicking water.

'All these baths Henry gives Dad. You reckon he's baptizing him all the time?'

Mum wrings out her flannel, puffing a bit.

'I thought you only got it once,' she says. 'Any more questions, Morton Flack?'

'Will that scar always be there, where they cut his throat open?'

'Some things never go away.'

After tea and all the praying and reading and doing the Lord's Supper with sherry and bread, we drag Dad out onto the verandah to watch the sun go down. Grammar sings to herself in her room. Tegwyn goes in and plays the piano hard like she's poking all its teeth out.

We sit out here and see the night coming, and wait for Henry Warburton. Mozzies come around. The light up on the house shows the eyes at the edge of the forest, but Henry Warburton doesn't show.

Mornings and nights go past. Tegwyn won't talk. She beats the piano up and it makes these kind of yells that are music. Maybe Henry Warburton isn't coming back, like he's baptized us and now he's off for good. Just dumped God all over us. Things are bad, real bad. Everyone's thinking the same thing, I reckon. And Christmas getting closer, and Dad so heavy to carry to the bath every day.

'You think we could wash him in bed?' I say to Mum as we go in to get him.

'He's not in hospital now,' she says. 'Sam Flack can take a bath like any normal man.'

Every day we drag him out. I don't sleep good. Worse than normal. All night I lie on my bed, looking up at the daddy-long-legs hanging off my reading light. Makes you feel like the only person left in the world, like everyone else is dead. Sometimes I read the story about the Pommie kids going through the wardrobe into a strange land, and once I even try myself; I get in my wardrobe and close the door and wait, but all that happens is the stink of old socks makes me want to sick up.

In the days I help Mum or muck around in the forest or down at the creek. And some nights when I don't sleep and can't think myself away, I get up and walk quiet around the house to check on everyone. I go down the hall and look in on Tegwyn. Her light is still on. Through a hole I see her on the bed. In her mouth is a smoke. A *smoke*! She sucks on it and makes kind of smoke doughnuts that go up to the ceiling and squash flat. She has no clothes on, sitting there smoking. On her tits there's red marks – all over – like she's got chicken pox or something. She has another puff. I wonder if I should tell. No. Real careful she takes the smoke out of her mouth and looks at the hot end and puts it on one tit and shivers. Burning! Oh, geez. Oh, geez. I go down the hall and out the back and a bit of sick comes up. I don't get it. I don't. Why does she do things like that? Why is she unhappy all the time? Why does she hate us?

'Is that you, Lil Pickering?'

I go inside and see Grammar. I sit next to her and pick up her old yellow hand from off the sheet.

'Who you listening for, Grammar? Who you hearing all the time?' She snores. In olden days she must have been beautiful, old Gram. And her music, too. She was married to a policeman, that was my Grampa who I never saw. Dad says they lived in country towns all over. Margaret River, Bridgetown, Manjimup, York. He kept getting transferred and she went with him, playing the music and having babies. That's Dad's brothers and sisters. Not worth a zac, he reckons.

'Is? Is . . .?'

'Who's there, Gram?'

'Walking near . . . oh, biscuits . . . jam . . .'

I go up the hall and check on Mum and Dad. They have the sheet down. Mum has Dad's hand on her belly.

I go back to bed. I take the Bible off the kitchen table with me. I turn my light on. The daddy-long-legs runs off. I read for a bit to get sleepy.

You are beautiful, my darling, as Tirzah,
lovely as Jerusalem,
majestic as troops with banners.
Turn your eyes from me;
they overwhelm me.
Your hair is like a flock of goats
descending from Gilead.
Your teeth are like a flock of sheep
coming up from the washing.

What a poem! This bloke taking the Michael out of his girlfriend for being ugly and for dropping her falsies in the washing. What a book. Stories! Pompous Pilot, Juders, Holly Ghosts. Doesn't get me sleepy at all.

Christmas Eve comes slow enough, waiting out on the verandah each night after tea, but it gets here. Mum is so tired when she gets up, she can't stop crying. We try to get Dad out the bed for his bath before breakfast because there's lots to do for tomorrow. But we're too tired and Mum can't stop crying. So I get the wheelchair. I jam me fingers in it trying to open it and that makes Mum cry worse. We get Dad in it, and wheel him down the hall with Mum blubbering on him. She hates the wheelchair.

I pray at breakfast. 'Jesus fix us up. We're breaking to bits here. Make us happy tomorrow on your birthday, Amen.' Mum pours big cups of sherry for the Lord's Supper and we are a bit happier. Then she starts cooking the cakes and I go out to do the chooks for tomorrow.

Not so bad when you've done it before. I kill two chooks with the machete. I'm holding a chook with no head, letting the blood go on the dirt, when I look across and see a big, high, green truck at the roadhouse and men bringing mattresses and chairs out to it. Out the front is a FOR SALE sign. I see Fat carrying a box and I look away.

All day you can smell cakes and bickies cooking. By late in the day, the Cherrys have gone, moved away. I go over and do something I can't stop. I piddle under their back door. I used to piddle in the middle of the road at night, going round and round like a drill. It made a piss ring that dried and would stay there three days. Don't know why I used to do it, but. Piddling under the Cherrys' door is worse, but I don't stop – just keep hosing it under. Then I snoop around the back for a bit, looking at the pieces of newspaper under the clothesline, an old shoe, the empty bit of dunny roll. And then I see something for Mum and grab it and carry it back real careful.

After tea we bring out Dad and even Grammar onto the verandah. No one says anything. Tegwyn sits on her legs with her eyes closed. I listen hard to the forest. Think I hear something. Yes. A bell. A bell ringing: *bong, bong,* in the forest. I've heard it before.

'Can you hear that bell?' I ask everyone.

'More crap from you,' Tegwyn says.

'Bell?' says Mum, kind of ratty.

'Yeah, hear it?'

'Oh, that.'

'You *hear* it?' I can't believe it. Someone else gets my visions.

'It's a big piece of steel or something down at the mill, Ort,' Mum says, like she's got no time for this. 'It bangs around in a westerly. Used to give me the willies once.'

I can't say anything. It hurts, you know. I don't say one thing. All me guts goes tight and hot.

For a long time it's just quiet out here on the verandah.

'Well, this is bloody cheerful,' Tegwyn says.

'Tegwyn, please –'

'Happy Christmas, everyone!'

'Let's . . . let's sing carols, then,' Mum says. She's almost bawling.

'Oh, Gawd.'

'Well, what do you suggest, Miss Smarty Pants? You got any better ideas? You got any ideas at all in your bloody selfish head? Life isn't tailor-made just for you, you know! There's other people to consider here. Sick people. Tired people. There's better people than you here.'

Tegwyn stands up. 'Go to hell. I'm getting a job.'

'What, you're gonna wait in your room till a job comes out here asking you to do it?'

'I hate your guts,' Tegwyn says. 'You're weak in the head, pathetic. You're a hick, a burnt-out hippy from the olden days. And now you're born-again, bashing the Bible and Holy Jesus. I think you're crap.'

Mum's face is moving in the dark. You can see it jumping around. 'Come here,' she says. Tegwyn stays put. 'Come here, please, Tegwyn.' Tegwyn is smiling.

'Okay, beat me up. Make bruises on me, make blood come out everywhere. Show 'em how pathetic you are.' Then she walks across to Mum with a white smile in the dark. Mum stands up. I squint, wait for it. Suddenly, Mum grabs her and her arms go round her hard so you can hear the air coming out of Tegwyn. Mum's hands lock like they'll need bolt-cutters to undo. She squeezing.

'I love you,' Mum says. 'I love you. Love you. Love you.' And then Tegwyn is bawling and all saggy and smaller-looking, and they stay like that for a long time.

Later we sing 'Silent Night' and it makes me sad. In my brain I can see Jesus getting born, but I can't see his face. In the end I give him my face. Could be worse for him; there's uglier people than me.

The bell rings. That light still glows. I have a bit of a bawl in the second verse.

Christmas. We give our presents. It's pretty weak, this year. Mum gives me Dad's walking hat, the one with the budgie feathers in it. She gives Tegwyn a brooch; I've seen it before, it's one of hers. I give Tegwyn the black smooth stone I found down at the creek once. We both get real embarrassed. I give Dad the tools in the pillowslip and the Pirelli calendar – Mum looks like she's gonna chuck a wobbly until I go out and get her present. It's the sunflower I pinched from the back of the roadhouse. She kisses me. She cries. Now I know for sure – we really haven't got much money. The Dole isn't a lot of money.

Mum puts the chooks in the oven and I scrub the fresh little spuds and Tegwyn picks peas; it starts to smell like Christmas. I bring Grammar and Dad into the loungeroom. The stove growls.

Suddenly there's a bang from somewhere. We all stop what we're doing. A car noise. I go outside, and down the long drive comes a yellow car, old and farting, rolling down the drive towards me, and there he is – Henry Warburton at the wheel.

'Well, Morton, old son,' he says, pulling into the shade behind the house, his elbow out the window, 'what do you reckon?'

'It's a heap.'

'Cut it out, it's an original 1958 FC Holden Special.'

Mum and Tegwyn come out. Mum is wiping her hands on the hem of her dress and you can see all her legs. Tegwyn walks like she's in no hurry for anyone. Henry Warburton gets out and leans against the 1958 FC Holden Special. It groans a bit, sniffs, and ticks. It stinks of burning oil. The back door is wired on with coathangers. The red seats are all furry and busted. The tyres are balder than babies' bums.

'Where the hell have you been?' Mum says, real quiet and angry.

'Doing business,' Henry Warburton says with a smile. He looks clean, with new clothes on. 'Working on your behalf, I might say.'

'What've you done?' Mum looks real worried and nearly as old as Mrs Cherry. 'Where'd you get this heap of rubbish?'

'No one's taken to the old FC yet, I see.'

'It's a heap of crap,' Tegwyn says.

'I sold the wreck of Sam's ute and bought this.'

'But how . . . without . . . because . . . papers and things –'

'All organized.'

'How?'

'Today, people, we're all going on an outing. It's Christmas Day, day of rest and rejoicing, day of contemplation – though not too exhaustive – and day of thanking the Lord for what is. Where to, kids?'

'The reservoir,' Tegwyn says.

'Yeah,' I say, 'the reservoir.'

'But lunch isn't ready,' Mum says, kind of smiling.

'We'll take it with us,' he says.

'Let's do it!' Tegwyn yells.

'At least wait until it's cooked,' Mum says.

'Righto,' Henry Warburton says as he puts up the bonnet.

New pine forests pass by. Henry Warburton's 1958 FC Holden Special farts and rattles and takes us up the road real slow, but it's enough to make you feel rich anyway. Bees splat on the windscreen; honey gurps out of them and spreads in the wind. The smell of hot grass comes in the windows. There's the smell of Christmas lunch all wrapped in tea-towels in the cardboard box on my knees. The wind gets in Grammar's hair and it goes all grey and white everywhere so you can't see how old she is. Dad is next to her, awake and blinking in the wind. His shirt is yellow, flapping, with the sun on it. I muck around with the ashtray that's in the back of the seat. There's butts and ash and bits of lolly paper in it and a mean kind of smell. I look at the back of the heads in front. Henry Warburton's hair is flat-greasy with snowy bits of white sticking to it and getting on his shoulders. He's singing and thumping the wheel. Tegwyn's hair is down and kinky from being plaited, and pouring all over the seat with little worms and snakes of it dancing in the wind and tickling my nose. I can see over her shoulder she's mucking around with knobs and vents and things. Mum's hair is down too and brushed; it looks like white wood and smells good enough to eat.

We turn off onto a smaller road and go downhill where trees are thick and shady and make big pools of shade on the road. Silver water. The dam. Brown stones. Some barbecues. And no one around at all. Next to the water, in the shade, we spread tarps and blankets and bring out the box and Dad and Grammar, and Henry Warburton has four bottles of beer. He says a prayer and flicks the tops off. We lie back, push Dad and Grammar back to back and get into it. Birds go mad in the trees and the water flashes and the ants come and everyone is eating and laughing and sighing and blowing the white off the top off their beer with gravy under their noses and peas in their laps. Wishbones, the parson's nose, baked spuds, long burps, and me guts sticks out like I swallowed the 1958 FC Holden Special itself.

III

Chapter Thirteen

I sit up in bed so fast it cracks my back. He's screaming, calling out. Fall out of bed. Down the hall to the closed door of the loungeroom where Henry Warburton still sleeps, ever since Christmas. Put my eye to the keyhole, and there he is, on his mattress in the raw with his sheet kicked down and his old fella sticking up like a flagpole again, and in the moonlight there's tears on his face, and he says real quiet:

'Go away.'

I step back from the door.

'No. Away.'

Can he see me?

'Bobo. Oh God! No. Hmph!'

I go back to bed and lie down and watch the light from the full moon and the cloud on the roof come pouring in through the curtains like it's milk from a bucket. What makes me think milk is the cow Henry Warburton bought for us. She's called Margaret and she's brown and white with big tits hanging down. I'm learning to get the milk out of 'em. When you got your ear against her belly when you're pulling milk out, you can hear sounds you'd think came from *Star Wars*. Ooowup-wup-wup . . . owkss-ut . . . gbolp . . . reeet. It's like cows talk five languages in their three guts.

Six weeks we've had Margaret. Mum reckons we're all getting fat from the cream. Dad's drinking it with a straw. At least he's doing that much. Henry Warburton sells things, bits of stuff from the sheds, to buy feed.

Down the highway we go in the 1958 FC Holden Special, farts, squeaks, smoke and all, three of us across the front seat like real hoons with our elbows out the windows. If there was a radio we'd have it going flat-chat, boy. Down the highway, through Bankside, past the paddocks full of stumps, and down to where you can see the city going all the way to the sea.

'I think you're supposed to go to your nearest suburban office,' Henry Warburton says. 'I know. I've been on the dole more times than you've pouted at yourself in the mirror.'

'I don't care,' Tegwyn says. 'I wanna go to the big one in town. I don't wanna work in the foothills or out on the limits. I wanna get a job in the city, in the offices, the skyscrapers.'

'Regardless –'

'Look,' she says, putting her feet up on the dash, 'you said you'd take me. Anyway, this car belongs to the Flacks. Me and Small Thing here are Flacks – that's two against one.'

So we go all the way in, through the places where there's houses and lawns and cars in cement drives, and trees all along the roads, past factories and streets and streets of car yards with little plastic flags out front, to where you can't see anything but walls and windows and red-orange-green lights and people walking and cars bumpered up as far as you can see.

And then up in this car park that's like the inside of a big cake, round and round, up and up, until we get to the roof in the sun and find a spot. We get out and look across the city. The river is fat and blue and buildings come up white out of the ground like they're brand-new.

'Let's go,' Henry Warburton says.

'Wish Mum was here,' I say.

'She hates the city,' Henry Warburton answers.

'Alright by me,' says Tegwyn. Her jeans are so tight you can nearly read the size of her undies.

'I don't wanna be a bloody check-out-chick at Woolworths!'

'That's if you're lucky,' Henry Warburton says as we get into the 1958 FC Holden Special.

'Are we still going to the beach?' I ask, putting me feet up on the glovebox.

'Shut your face, Small Thing.'

'Your sister is learning slowly, Ort, that her services aren't in any more demand than those million and a half others who're trying to get a job. But don't worry,' he says with a laugh, 'she knows what she's on about. She's an adult now.'

'Up your bum, preacher.'

Henry Warburton winks at me and starts the car. 'I think the beach would be lovely, Ort. Might even cool someone off.'

The beach is the whitest flaming thing you've ever seen in your life! Black car parks, green water, and white sand that goes for miles. You squint as you walk across it, through oily brown people on blankets and under brollies with radios going and babies crying. Some girls with their boobs showing, brown things with eyes that watch you go past. Geez.

Tegwyn and me get in the water with a run and a dive like all the other people are doing. I come up with me mouth full of sand and me nose all skinned. We swim out to where everyone is standing. It's quiet and flat and people talk, but they're always looking out to sea. Maybe they're looking for Rottnest. Tegwyn and me duck-dive and swim around. Tegwyn stands on her hands so her legs come out the water and people whistle. Then the whole place goes mad. People swimming out to sea, wading, paddling at the water with their hands. Blokes on surfboards turning round and going like hell. Takes me a while to see the big lines coming in like a convoy of wheat trucks, some with bits of white blowing back off the top like wheat dust coming off the load.

The first wave lifts me off my feet and puts me down again. I hear it thump behind me but I don't look 'cause this other one's coming. And two behind it. The second one makes me kick like crazy to climb over. The third one drops on me like the side of a house. There I am on the bottom, with sand in me gob and water thumping me up and down on the back, turning me in circles so I don't know me left from me right, and me lungs saying: 'Get up, Morton Flack, you dill. Get out of the water or you'll die!' And in the end, without doing anything, I pop up, head-first, with all this white stuff around like the soap bubbles from the washing, and Tegwyn is laughing her box off next to me. It tastes funny. Like blood. It's crook water!

Everyone else catches the waves when they come. They swim with them and shoot along to the beach. But I stay put. I get run over by surfboards. I get run over by fat ladies with prickly legs. I get run over by bigger waves. I get run over by my own sister. And then I reckon I've had enough. I think all the knocks have ruined my brains, 'cause I turn around and catch the next wave that's coming. I kick and go freestyle like mad. The wave comes up behind me like a brick wall. Then I'm flying. Really flying. Most of me isn't even in the wave. I'm hanging out over a sandbar that's a long, long way down and I hear me own voice going: 'Oooooohhhh!' Like jumping out of a tree. Onto your head. Hohh! I come up with more sand down my throat and music in my head and another wave tumbles me over. Another one fills me up with water and sends me along the bottom. The last one drops me on the beach. I get up and then I know. Me shorts! Here I am standing in the middle of the city with nothing on. Henry Warburton is there, laughing.

'Had an accident, old son?'

There's people everywhere, looking. Never seen so many eyes in all me life. I walk. My legs are all wobbly. Feels like I been run over by a truck.

'Here.' Henry Warburton takes off his shirt and ties it round me. We walk up the beach and sit on the towels. I kind of feel numb. For a long time I sit watching more waves come. Water runs out my nose. Next to us, a girl rubs oil on her boobs and makes them move in funny ways and it gives me goosebumps, like when you scratch a blackboard with your fingernail. Henry Warburton is looking too. I can feel it.

'Dirty old sods.'

I look up real quick. It's Tegwyn, dripping, wiping snot from her chin. I get up off her towel, and then she looks at me and sneers.

'Got a rock in your pocket, Ort?'

I look down. Out the front of the shirt Henry Warburton lent me, there's the outline of my old fella sticking out like a handle. The girl next to us is smiling.

Then Henry Warburton takes a step, and *slap!* across Tegwyn's face and her eyes go wide and full and then she's off, running up the beach towards the carpark, kicking sand all over people, her bum jiggling; people whistle and hoot and Henry is after her, calling: 'Tegwyn, Tegwyn, listen, I –'.

So here I am standing in the middle of a million eyes with this thing sticking out like it's made up its mind to point rudely at people for the rest of its life.

'I wanna go to Kings Park,' I say as we drive along in the traffic, still wet and salty. Tegwyn isn't saying anything. Since Henry Warburton caught her out in front of the hamburger place, in front of all them people, and said how sorry he was and everything, she has not said one word.

'Why Kings Park?' he says, looking at me kind of strange.

'Oh, I just wanted to see it. I dunno.'

But he takes us. He's in a kind of mood where he has to; we could make him take us anywhere.

From Kings Park you can see the whole river and freeway and buildings and parks and causeway. This is where Mum and Dad got to know each other. This is a bit of the reason I'm here. This is a bit of me. I s'pose it's different at night, more . . . romantic? I can just see Mum and Dad coming out of them trees back there and coming onto this bit of grass with all the cannons pointed out towards where we live behind the hills, and him saying, 'You know, Alice Benson, when we get married, we'll go and live near trees like them. And our kids'll be called Ort and Tegwyn, and it's gonna be great.' All the lights, all the . . .

'Ort!' Henry says. 'Are you with us? Time to go, mate. Back to Flack country.'

I walk back to the 1958 FC Holden Special with a big grin on me face that a doctor couldn't get off.

'The breeze is in,' says Henry Warburton, looking at the trees bending as we creep along towards the hills.

'Fremantle Doctor,' I say, and just the words make me feel good and sad at the same time.

All the way up through the foothills, no one talks; it's a kind of sleepy, tired feeling, listening to the 1958 FC Holden Special squeaking and popping in second gear.

Chapter Fourteen

High school's getting closer, you know. Not that I'm worried about it, but. Bad enough going to high school at all, but there's not going to be one person there that I know. Fat is gone and he was the only kid in my school who's in my year. Last year I knew every single kid in our school (there's only ten). There's a thousand at Outfield High – that's what Tegwyn says. Three weeks. That's all. All I do now is muck around on me own, walking in the forest, playing armies, finding little creatures in the bush, talking to myself. and sometimes to God. Funny when you talk to God. He's like the sky (well, he is the sky, kind of). Never says anything. But you know he listens. Right down in your belly, even in your bum you know.

Yesterday I took the car roof down the creek to the bridge and back, but there was no fun in it. Fat's fatness was the best part of it – you didn't know when he was gonna capsize you. And it was someone to talk to and see things with. When you see something, a rabbit running away, a dugite in the grass, a fox watching you from a long way off, you say 'Look! Look at that!' Even when no one's there, you say it. Sometimes I hang around the back of Cherrys'. Sometimes I chase Margaret around. Sometimes she chases me. Sometimes I stay inside and read *Mad* comics.

Out there today Henry Warburton is walking Dad in the wheelchair, up and down the yard, all day, talking talking talking about I dunno what. I reckon Henry's got something crook that makes him yell out at night and go quiet sometimes. And there's those fits, and that speech thing that's gone away now. And his glass eye. He's taught us how to pray the Lord's Prayer. He teaches us little things. He's not that bad. He says things that are right. But he hit Tegwyn. Maybe he did it for me. She was ragging me in front of the whole city. But he never said anything. My heart works better than my brain. Me brain says Henry Warburton was sticking up for me, but me heart doesn't believe it, and when me heart makes up its mind, that's it.

Mum is kind of different these days. She doesn't seem so sad any more. You don't see her sitting out on the verandah crying over Dad and combing his hair with her fingers. She's wearing all her bright dresses with feathers and things in her hair. She wears the shell earrings she used to wear a long time ago. She looks young. She washes her hair a lot. She lets Henry Warburton have Dad to himself all day. It's good to see her happy, I s'pose. Can't tell if it's Jesus or Henry Warburton she's happy about. I wonder how long it will last.

Days and nights are the same for me now. Both kind of lonely. There's no one to hang around with.

Out there, Henry Warburton walks Dad up and down and Dad has this no-frown-no-smile look on his face like he can't do either. There's wheelmarks in the dirt that get deeper and deeper.

Some new people have moved in over the road. Makes you feel sorry for them, moving into that sad place. The man and lady came across this morning and said hullo. She had big teeth like fenceposts; they looked like they could chew steel. Her hair was all frizzy and grey and she smelt like lemons. He was tall and had a loopy back and he looked at you out the top of his head which was small as a softball. He didn't stink of anything. I thought he was alright, but *she* talked like she thought she was the king's bickies.

'Hel-loo. We are the Alfred Wat-sons. Wee have as-sumed proprietorship of the traaans-port establishment o-ver yon-der.' I dunno why she talked so funny. They look just as daggy as us. She said:

'Those previous owners must have been a tri-al for you people. Everything smells awfully of u-rine.' Mum and Henry talked with them a bit. Mum looked cocky again, like she used to. They looked at us like they were dead sure they weren't as daggy as us.

February. School tomorrow. And here I am out on the dunny for the sixth time tonight. My teeth chatter even though it's hot as hell. I sit here till it all runs out. Going past the bathroom I hear Henry Warburton talking, and stop.

'Hell, Sam, how can you listen to me day after day? Guess you don't have much choice. Sometimes I wonder if I'm not here for my own sake more than yours. You're the perfect priest, Sam. You don't believe, you listen, and you don't say anything. You . . . what the hell am I saying?'

I go to my room. He talks that kind of stuff all the time, and then he cries at night. He doesn't muck around much with me any more, doesn't play french cricket or anything. He argues with Tegwyn and wheels Dad up and down the yard and leaves me and Mum to ourself. And sometimes Mum looks at him, kind of hungry.

For a while I lie here on my bed trying not to think about tomorrow. Then I get up and go and listen at the bathroom door again.

'I know you're waiting, Sam. God is too, I can feel it. I'll do it, Sam. Soon. But I'm so scared, so . . .'

Talk talk talk. The other day Henry Warburton talked to Dad for so long the bath water went cold and Dad was shivering and blue and Mum came in and went crook something awful.

He only sometimes does the Lord's Supper with us now; after meals he goes and sits on his own, or takes Dad for a walk, or tries to teach Tegwyn something on the piano, and Mum and me are left to do it on our own.

Talk talk talk.

I go outside, walk right into the middle of the yard and look back at the house. That cloud-light is still there. Now that's a mystery. Little clouds that shine like moons don't sit on everyone's house. Or maybe they do and not everyone can see it. Mum can't see it. Not even Henry Warburton can see it. If you chuck stones at it they go right through – nothing happens. Every angle, it looks the same. It's like a dream that's always with you. But it's there – it's my vision. I know God's in it somewhere. He *is* waiting for something.

Bong! There goes that bell in the forest. Like a school bell. Yuk!

Not even the chooks are up yet, not even the birds, not even the sun, and here I am jogging around the house, lapping, going round like I'm tied to it, like I'm a model plane with feet going round and round on the same track. Jogging is the dumbest thing in the world to do. I can't think of anything dumber. Except eating olives and going to high school. Round I go again. Can see my own footprints in the dirt now. As I come around past the back verandah I see Mum in her sleeping tee-shirt of Dad's, standing there, rubbing her eyes. She looks at me and her eyes make me stop dead like there wasn't another step left in me anyway.

'Morton-flamin'-Flack, what the *hell* do you think you're doing?'

'Jogging, Mum.'

'*Jogging*? From my bed it sounded like a bloody stamp*ede*! Get inside, you'll give the world a fright.'

'But I'm nervous.'

'What the heck you wanna be nervous for? God looks after you, you know that.'

'He doesn't stop me going to the dunny fifty times a night.'

'We'll have to sew your bum up, then. Anything. Just don't surround the house with yourself at four o'clock in the morning.'

'I'll go for a walk.'

'Okay, do that, then.'

'You wanna come?' I say.

'At four o'clock in the morning?' She steps down off the verandah with her thongs clacking. 'I think the Lord must have been cracking a joke on us when he gave us children,' she says as we walk towards the forest. There's all crackly bits of sleep in her eyes, and her hair is all over. She knows how to love people. I can feel the warm from the bed still on her, and the smell of Dad, that Flack smell.

[118]

The forest has got the light in it that comes before the sun, and you can hear things moving in grass and bushes. We walk down past the creek and into the real thick part of the forest where it tumbles over the edge of the hill to a tricky slope where the loggers couldn't cut trees down. You can see the edge of the city in tiny bits between trees here.

'How come we live up here, Mum? Everyone else lives in the city.'

'I dunno. It's just where we are, I suppose. We liked the trees, your Dad and me. You know that.'

'How come we stay here if Tegwyn hates it?'

'Kids hate everything when they're sixteen. Even themselves. It was like that for me.'

I think about that for a while as the sun makes a dot of pink through the trees behind us. Then we make a turn and come around with the little pink point of sun in our eyes.

'What does God really look like, you reckon?'

'Why all the questions?'

'Get them all out the way before high school. Tegwyn said if you ask questions kids'll think you're a suckhole.'

'But you don't care what they think, do you?'

'Oh. No.' Funny how when you get older you can easy say things you don't mean.

'What does God look like then. Heck, Ort, you ask toughies,' she says, picking up a stick with a fork in the end and a black leaf skewered on it. 'Now. Henry was talking about this a while back. He said that no one has seen God except Jesus. No one else knows what he looks like. He always comes with something to cover himself up. Like people couldn't handle it if he showed his real self. Remember that story about the whirlwind and the one about the burning bush? We'll see him soon enough. When we're in heaven.'

'Are you still into it?' I ask, squinting as that pink sun gets stronger.

'Into what?'

'This believing.'

'Well, yeah.'

'I just wasn't sure.'

Mum smiles. 'We don't know much about it all, do we? It's made us different, Ort, this believing. It's like we weren't even alive before. It doesn't stop us hurting. But . . . but you know the hurting's gonna stop one day. Everything's gonna make sense. One day we'll understand.'

I break off a dead stick and suck the end. 'Why don't we go to a church? Is that what people do?'

'I s'pose so. Never thought of it. There's that sign in the drapery. Gospel meeting, they call it. The one the Watkinses run.'

'But they don't like us. I heard Mrs Watkins talking about us. Called us hippies. What's hippies?'

'It's people who lived in the olden days. Don't worry about it.'

'I'm not worried.'

'You? Course not. It's normal for you to go to the dyke fifty times a night. Morton Flack never worries.'

'I don't wanna go today.'

'You have to.'

'That's why I don't wanna.'

The school bus is an old tub. Fifteen kids all sit up the back. I sit up behind the driver. The bus crawls down the long hill in low. In my bag there's a lunch box, a *Mad* comic and a tennis ball. Some kids up the back are smoking. Don't they know it kills you? Big globs of slag come down the aisle. I read my *Mad* comic, or just make out I am, till the bus gets to Outfield High.

The school is down at the bottom of the foothills where the city has crept out to take over the country. There's some parts with houses all together, and parts with chook farms or flower farms and some factories. When I see the high school me heart goes blah. Looks like a gaol. Two storeys high, all brown from bore water, people with bags walking around like they're in for life.

Well, then it starts. Everyone is looking for melons. You can tell the melons. We all look scared to death, some of us have shorts on, and we're all in little groups on the oval. I don't know anybody. I've got no one to make a group with, so I have a look around, keep walking like I know where I'm going to, like I'm a group of my own. Girls with pink hair point at me. Classroom doors everywhere. I go up to the drinking taps and put my head under so it's all wet. But it's no good – further down the quadrangle four big kids yell: 'Melon!' and drag me in the dunnies and pick me up and shove my head in the crappiest bowl and flush. They pinch my *Mad* comic and my tennis ball and nick off. Another gang of kids push some melon into the pisser and I take off.

I'm late for five classes. I get lost seven times. Someone calls me a poofter and a teacher tells me to get me hair cut. I get flushed again just after the last bell.

Mum bawls when I get home and tell her. I stink like hell. Tegwyn laughs. I stay under the shower till I half turn into a prune.

All week it's the same. I go for runs in the morning to get ready for being called a poofter and being told by old poopheads to cut my hair. The bus ride is awful, kids killing 'emselves up the back with smokes, pink-haired girls showing me their braces. I get everywhere late and have to do scab duty at morning recess. Scab duty is picking up wet tissues and brown apple cores in the quadrangle. Mr Frost sends a letter home to Mum telling her to get my hair cut. Mum writes one back telling him to mind his own business. I do scab duty a lot. I don't listen much in class. It's hot and flies sing you to sleep, and I always think about swimming in the creek.

The second week is the same. And the third week. The fourth week I'm used to it. And Mum gets me some long pants, so that's something. Home at nights I do some of my homework and then sit out on the verandah with everyone else, but it's not the same anymore. I feel different. I feel like I live out in the middle of nowhere. I pray to God and hope he hears me. All I get is deadly quiet from him. I'm kind of stuck. I don't feel like a kid anymore. I'm not even a proper teenager. I'm not a grown-up adult. I'm not in the city. I'm not properly in the country. I dunno what the hell to do with meself.

Sometimes I stand out in the forest after dark, thinking about me poor crippled Dad, and the way Mum is . . . I dunno . . . not the same, and how I find Henry Warburton out behind the sheds sometimes, saying through his teeth, 'Help me, damn you. Do something.' And him not saying much to me these days, and him wheeling the old man up and down like a bloke who's waiting for someone to come and get him. When I'm standing out there, thinking of all those things, it all looks pretty bad, the whole show. Mum said it would this year. It's puberty or some dumb thing. Everything is just so dumb. Sometimes, some nights, it's just so stupid. And I just go out and look back at the house, and that little cloud of light that came on the house the day they brought Dad back, it stops me from bawling. It makes me stop everything. Something in it says to me, says to me soul in me belly and in me bum, *Hang on, Morton Flack.*

Crazy, eh?

Chapter Fifteen

Sunday morning. It's cool. Summer is about over. Margaret makes ork, pork, goilk noises in her guts. Her milk comes out hard and thin and makes the bucket growl. I can see sparrows watching us from the window ledge. I wonder if cows like their tits pulled. Margaret always comes whingeing up to the back door for it. She eats Tegwyn's undies on the clothesline like it's just for something to do. Glad Henry Warburton didn't bring us a goat.

When I take the milk in, Mum says to me:

'Why don't we go to the Watkinses' church this morning? It's good to go to church, isn't it?'

'I dunno,' I say, pouring off the milk into the big pot on the stove, 'I s'pose.'

'It says where two or three are gathered . . . where two or three . . . something something . . . oh, whatever. Henry, what do you think?'

Henry Warburton shrugs and doesn't look up from his newspaper. He gets them from Bankside now, tries to get me to read 'em. Not even the comic section is any good.

'Henry?'

Henry Warburton looks up. 'If you'd like to.'

'Is that to say you're not coming?'

'Well, obviously you can't take Sam and his mother, and someone's got to look after them.'

Mum thinks for a bit.

'Tegwyn will look after them, won't you love?'

'Always me,' Tegwyn says. 'Why the hell should I?'

'I'll stay,' Henry Warburton says.

'Maybe you'll be able to teach my daughter some manners.'

'I don't think there's any hope of that,' he says with a grin.

The sun is out but it's kind of cool. When we go inside the back part of the drapery shop that Mr and Mrs Watkins run, it's like walking into a fridge. It's a kind of storeroom where the rows of chairs are. Up front there's a table with a lacy table cloth that looks like it's got a big parcel under it. On the wall is a flag, the Australian flag. There's a reading-stand-thing up there, too, and a picture of the baby Jesus. I count nine people. Everyone talks in whispers like they don't wanna wake up baby Jesus. They all look like they're going to a dance or something; all got their best clothes on, and there's me and Mum in our thongs. We sit down at the back. Mr Watkins gives us a little blue book and a big thin book. They got songs in them. Hymns.

'What's hymens mean?' I whisper in Mum's ear.

'Hims. It's hims,' she says. A lady is looking at me all red. 'Just old time songs, Ort.'

Hims. Makes me wanna giggle.

'Welcome! Welcome! Welcome! Here we are, it's the Lord's Day and here we are in the Lord's House, so let's offer unto him our prayers.' Everyone closes their eyes and holds their noses with their fingers like they got a headache. Everyone bends over like they dropped something on the floor. 'We praise and thank Thee our Father that Thou has given unto us plenty . . .' He goes on in this funny talk, like he comes from another planet and talks a little bit like us, but not enough to let us understand right. Thee and Thou. Dunno where they fit in, but the bloke up there in the blue suit and oily hair knows 'em pretty well.

'The text for today, brethren and sisters, is taken from the book of Revelation, chapter sixteen. Ahem. Hurumph.

'And I heard a great voice out of the temple saying to the seven angels, Go your ways, and pour out the vials of the wrath of God upon the earth. And the first went, and poured out his vial upon the earth; and there fell a noisome and grievous sore upon the men which had the mark of the beast and upon them which worshipped his image . . .'

Geez. On and on. This gutsy story with drinking blood and scorching and earthquakes and no reason for it. Then Mr Watkins gets up with his blue suit and his hair oiled too, and he stands behind the table and starts talking about the Lord's Supper which me and Mum know about. He tells a little story that I don't get, and then he takes off the lacy tablecloth and there's two trays. He passes one to two blokes in blue suits who pass it to each other across the row. When they get to our row they stop passing and go back to the front. Mum looks at me. There's only us in our row.

'Only crackers, anyway,' she says. 'Can't be doing too well with the drapery.' A lady with fruit in her hat looks around.

Then the other tray, full of little glasses, comes up and down the rows. This time Mum leans across the row in front when the tray goes past and she picks out two little glasses. When she sits down again, she gives me one. I drink it. The fruit lady gives us a dangerous look. Her apples go redder.

'It's only grapejuice!' I say. I look up. Everyone in the room is looking at us. The men passing the tray are red in the face.

'And I thought *we* were poor,' Mum says with a giggle.

Then they bring round another plate that people put little envelopes on.

'What is it?' I ask Mum. 'Letters? Don't they *say* their prayers to God?'

'Sshh!' the lady in front says. Her moustache goes all stiff at me. Her fruit jiggles.

This time the plate comes to us. Mum smiles and passes it to the man in the blue suit and oily hair who is still red in the face.

All the ladies have got hats on. Some with flowers in them. Some like cowboy hats. Some like crash helmets. Some like little pink zits on the top of their head.

Then Mrs Watkins warms up her accordion and everyone sings:

[125]

The Son of God goes forth to war,
A kingly crown to gain,
His blood-red banner streams afar:
Who follows in his train?
Who best can drink his cup of woe
Triumphant over pain . . .

Mrs Watkins has an orange dress on, and her arms are all orange too. They squeeze and push and the accordion sounds a bit like our 1958 FC Holden Special.

After the singing, the first man with a blue suit and oily hair gets up and shouts at us. It's like algebra and arithmetic and geography and story-time all wrapped into one. There's 666 and dragons and beasts and seven heads and four angels and 144,000 and Babylon and Russia and China and a thousand years and seven seals and Sodom and Gog and Magog and Mr Arafat and Com-munism and Blasphemia and Lambs and more blood drinking.

'Read the signs! Read-the-signs! The Antichrist himself comes. We have no doubt of it. The prophecies are fulfilled daily. For all nations have drunk of the wine of the wrath of fornication with her . . . the fornication of Babylon. John's own words from Patmos. We-have-no-*time*! The-need-is-*great*! *Press*ing. *Urgent*. How will we stand in the *tri*bulation? How? How? How will we stand in that time of woe and *tur*moil and crushing of spirits? How?'

The man shouts at us like he's angry, especially at us up the back. But I don't know what he means. He asks us questions and before we can answer he asks another one.

Real sudden, Mum stands up and jerks me up and pulls me along the row of empty chairs and just at the door on the way out she turns around and says:

'You don't have to shout. We're not animals, you know. And not even God's animals should be shouted at like they're made of mud!'

And then we're outside and we get in the car and Mum rests her head on the steering wheel and sighs. The horn goes on. The men in blue suits and oily hair come to the door and point their red faces at us.

When we get home Margaret has got into the vegetable patch and is trying out the tomatoes and treading on everything else. Dad is stuck out in the driveway on his own in the wheelchair, and Henry Warburton and Tegwyn are in the kitchen fighting.

'Don't try your religious crap on me, boy. Don't come the crapper with me. You just leave me alone, you big gawky galoot!'

Henry is standing by the stove, dodging all the lemons she's chucking at him, smiling away, shrugging his shoulders. Mum just goes real angry through the flying lemons to her room. I go out to Dad.

'Hi,' I say, taking off the brake and wheeling him down the drive. His hair is growing back and there's a good beard on him that makes him look old and real wise. I put my hand on the back of his head and feel how warm it is from the sun. The wheels crackle in the dirt. At the end of the driveway near the road, I turn him around and then I walk around and sit on the dirt in front of him. I look at his face. It's a good face, not real handsome, but straight — a telling-the-real-truth face. He looks kind of old and wise sitting there with his PJ's on. I reckon that's what God looks like. Dad's eyes look like they see everywhere today, all over the world.

I look up at the faded sky with its warty-looking moon. It goes on forever up there.

'Do it, God,' I say. 'Make him get up and walk.'

I sit back on the warm brown dirt and wait. And Dad sits there waiting, too. Birds land in the trees close by. They watch us. A little wind comes across, makes the leaves go silly. I keep waiting. The bush just sits there. The whole world goes on. Margaret moos like mad up behind the house 'cause no one's bothered to milk her. And nothing here changes. Then, after a long time Mum starts calling us in for tea.

When I get up it's nearly dark and Dad's shivering and I feel scared as hell.

Chapter Sixteen

Two weeks. Three weeks. Every day after school I take Dad out to the end of the driveway with a blanket on his legs 'cause it's getting cool, and every day I pray. Every day I wheel him back in for tea.

Homework. Here I am sitting in my room trying to write an essay on the Prime Minister, and it starts raining. Rain! It just comes out of nowhere, belting down on the tin roof. I get up and go into the hallway. Across the hall Henry Warburton is talking to Dad. I put my ear against the door, have to listen real hard because of the rain noise.

'. . . they used to annoint the sick person with oil, and lay hands on him and pray. I've never known you as your real self, Sam. I'm afraid. I'm a weak man, Sam.'

I go outside to the verandah and see the ground boiling in the dark. The light on the house makes milk ribbons in it.

And then it's April, real sudden. April Fool's Day I get told the principal Mr Whipper wants to see me in his office. I go to his office and say who I am. He looks at me kind of strange.

'Is this a poor joke?' he says.

'No, sir,' I say, nearly crapping myself.

'What did I want to see you for?'

'I thought you'd know, sir.'

'You are insolent, Mr Flack.'

'You mean you didn't want to see me?'

He doesn't wanna see me. I get six of the best to show how much he doesn't wanna see me. April Fool. Beaudy.

Henry Warburton works on the old Chev in the evenings. He works real late, banging, shouting, trying to get it to go. One of us goes to the back door every now and then to listen for the sound of the engine. It would really be something to hear that Chev after all these years of waiting. Like raising the dead, it'd be. But there's nothing.

Flowers have come out with the rain. Tiny yellow and pink ones all over and specially thick in the forest. On Saturday I follow Tegwyn into the forest and keep a long, long way back. She sings to herself and it's like the trees drink it up. I keep low and follow the pink of her jeans. She picks flowers and puts them in a bag. She looks so happy, picking flowers; never seen my sister Tegwyn so happy, and singing some dumb song that doesn't mean anything much. Makes me happy to follow her round.

I follow her back to the house. Henry is building a bigger fence for the vegetables. Some twenty-eights fly over, green as grass, looking for places to nest. Mum is washing. I let Tegwyn go inside with her little bag of flowers. Then I go in to see what she's up to. She looks like she's up to something. I walk real careful down the hallway. Look into Grammar's room. Grammar is asleep on her own. No one in my room. Tegwyn isn't in hers. Real careful I put my ear to the wall outside Dad and Mum's room.

'How's that, then, old boy?' she's saying. The door is half open. I look through the crack next to the GET THEM OUT OF VIET-NAM sticker, and there is Dad with all pink and yellow flowers in his hair. He looks like a king or a prince or something. I can't help meself; I burst in and say:

'Oh, Tegwyn, it's beautiful.'

She goes all stiff with pink and yellow flowers in her hands, and already her face is changing.

'It's lovely,' I say.

'It's a heap of crap,' she says, and pulls the flowers out, ripping at Dad's hair, chucks them into the box, opens the window and dumps 'em all out.

Later, Henry Warburton brings in some flowers for Mum and she goes all silly.

'This thing with Bobo Sax, Sam. Ngth. It was like nothing else you've ever been through in your life. She was like a bitch in heat. She was filthy. She stank. She never came out of that hut and I used to go to her. I'd hate myself. I hated her, but I'd go into that hut and sometimes I wouldn't come out for days. She was slippery, lithe, she had you like a vise. I tell you, that woman, that creature fed on my weakness. I drank and smoked myself into it. I forgot myself and my place, sometimes, and I was happy. But I'd wake up in that filthy, foul darkness sometimes, ngth, and want to tear myself to pieces.

'They said she was a witch, the local people. Maybe they were right, I don't know. That's why they burnt the place . . . after she was dead. Why do I need you for a priest, Sam? Why do I need a priest at all?'

He leaves Dad in the bath a long time these days. It's getting colder. He's gonna make him worse.

Sometimes instead of my homework I go through the back of that big black Bible of Henry Warburton's where it lists the words. I keep going back to OIL. I read all the stories about it, how they put it on people's heads who were kings, and how it was like gold and people argued over it. And here's this bit that Jesus' brother wrote down. Henry Warburton showed Mum a long time back.

Is any one of you in trouble? He should pray. Is anyone happy? Let him sing songs of praise. Is any one of you sick? He should call the elders of the church to pray over him and anoint him with oil in the name of the Lord. And the prayer offered in faith will make the sick person well; the Lord will raise him up. If he has sinned he will be forgiven. Therefore confess your sins to each other so that you may be healed. The prayer of a righteous man is powerful and effective.

Oil's what you do chips in. Oil's what those blokes at the drapery had in their hair.

The first night it's cold enough, I light a fire in the lounge room. Makes me feel good. I was born in this room with one ripper fire going. Mum irons clothes. She's real angry still about that church. She says she's tired of taking crap from people. We look at the busted telly every now and then. There's a funny story about that telly. It's been bust for two years. When Grammar was okay, when she used to help Mum with the cleaning and the cooking and the two of 'em used to laugh together, she had this thing about the telly. She hated it. Used to shout at Mike Walsh and Bert Newton. 'You don't fool me!' she used to say to them. 'It's all fake. Fakers!' It used to make us all laugh because it's true. On TV they all pretend. But soon Grammar started to get sick and inside herself. One day she came in when Mike Walsh was on and she got Mum's secateurs and started cutting up the back of the telly. The electricity chucked her into the fireplace. 'Do that to an old woman, will you? Shameless!'

'Henry's in there with Tegwyn again,' I say. 'What's he doing?'

Mum looks up from the steam. 'Trying to save her soul, I think. She's a hard nut, our Tegwyn.'

'She hates him.'

She nods.

'Do you like Henry?'

She flinches. Doesn't look up from her ironing. 'Oh, yeah.' Looks like she's got to thinking all of a sudden, like I knocked something out of place.

You can hear them shouting from here. At it all the time. In a while, Henry Warburton comes out and sits down by the fire. He covers his face. Looks like he's gonna cry, but no, he takes his hands away and he's taken one eye out and he's got it between his fingers, showing it to me.

'Henry, put it away, for goodness sake,' Mum says.

[132]

'See, Ort,' he says. 'This is like the eye of God.' He moves it all over the place. 'Sees everything.'

'I know what it sees.'

'Yes?'

'Bugger all.'

'Morton!' Mum says.

'That's glass. Doesn't see anything. God sees everything, and he's got two real eyes. I think you're full of crap. You don't even believe what you're talking about.'

The room is deadly quiet. Mum looks at me and then her face changes and she looks at Henry real cool. The fire crackles. Tegwyn is yelling from her room.

'Well how would you like to be called Tegwyn? How would you like to have to be out here in this dump living off yer own shitty vegies like a caveman? How would you like to look after children and crazies and cripples? How would you fucken like it?'

Henry gets up and goes outside.

After a while I get up and make some tea. The glass canisters along the shelf are full of eggs. *Eggs!* I go and get Mum. She looks but she doesn't see them. All she sees is rice and tea and flour and lentils. She goes back to the ironing. I make a pot of tea with those eggs looking down at me.

We sit and sip our tea and listen to the sound of breaking glass from the shed.

'He's busting up the Chev,' I say.

'Yes,' Mum says. She looks stuck, like she can't decide something.

And we drink our tea, and I just wonder what the hell's going on.

Chapter Seventeen

I stuff my essay on 'The Brave Anzacs at Gallipoli' into me schoolbag and Mum stuffs in a bag of Vegemite sangers. It's a rank essay; most of it I copied straight out of books I got from the library. The library at school is the only place I go to out of class. I even eat my lunch in there up between the L-Z shelves. There's books on trees and cars, other countries, even a big Bible with pictures. Sometimes I go to the encyclopaedia and look up the one on 'S'. It's nearly falling apart, the one on 'S'. Looks like a lot of kids want to know what the hell's going on you know where.

Anyway, I grab my bag, get a kiss from Mum, go out on the back verandah and there's Henry Warburton chucking up on the ground next to the 1958 FC Holden Special. He kind of yells as it comes up. Then he rests for a bit and looks at me, and then he wipes his mouth on a hanky and opens the car door and gets in. I go over and get in.

'You crook?'

He doesn't even look at me. The 1958 FC Holden Special drops its guts and we're off. All the way into Bankside he says nothing. I look at him a lot of the way; he's got this look on his face like he's scared. He's all bristly from not shaving and his eyes are red. His hair is greasy and all over. His clothes are dirty. I can smell the sick on him. He drops me off at Bankside outside the pub where some other kids wait. He doesn't even say goodbye.

I stand out close to the road away from the other kids. They're mostly older. It's boring, waiting for the bus. I look around. The pub and the drapers and the shop and up behind the pointy bit of the church. Boring. Over the road I see something moving. I look hard. It's a bobtail goanna. Looks crook, like it's trying to move but can't do it right. I go over and see that it's got one flat leg. Reckon it's been run over by a car. I pick him up. You can tell when a bobtail's real crook – it doesn't bite. He just looks at me and doesn't even open his mouth. I stuff him in me bag. The bus is coming.

All day I keep him in my bag. I check on him during every period, feed him bits of my sangers. Social studies and maths aren't so boring with a lizard in your bag. I call him Bartholemew 'cause it's in the Bible and it's a crazy name for a goanna to have. But by the last period it's shortened to Barry. With one leg flat as a popstick and mushy pink. I wrap a bit of Glad Wrap around it. Gonna fix this lizard up. I just sit there in English as Mrs Trigwell reads that dumb poem 'Jabberwocky' at us, laughing at herself all the way through, and I wait for school to be over. This school is full of kids who talk like people in the movies. They're not even like kids. Makes me feel like a baby.

Henry Warburton drives me home and doesn't even say hello.

'Do animals get into heaven?' I ask him.

He looks at me. 'S'pose so. Can't see why not.'

'Trees?'

'Probably.'

'Are you crook?'

He drives careful. Slow on the bends. He's had a shave and his clothes are clean, but it doesn't help much.

'Why?'

'You look rank.'

'Oh? Nngth.'

'You should pray about it.'

'Sure, Reverend.'

'I think there's something wrong with you.'

[136]

He looks at me with his eyes all red and a sad smile on him. 'God only knows what goes on in your brain, boy. Do they give you a hard time at school?'

'What do you mean?'

'For being . . . the way you are.'

'I stay in the library.'

'What're you gonna do when you bomb out?'

What's he mean? 'I dunno. Help Mum.'

'You're a singular sort.' He laughs. 'You are one in a million, boy. How did they make you?'

'In the bedroom,' I say. 'Sexual intercourse in the nude.'

He doesn't stop laughing all the way home. The 1958 FC Holden Special rattles and parps like it's laughing *its* box off, too.

I slip Barry under the wardrobe soon as I get home. Tea's on. Henry Warburton reads something short and prays something short. Mum dishes up the curry. I take some up to Grammar and feed her. When I come back Mum is talking.

'Sam and I built a pyramid out of logs before the kids were born. Out the back. Wasn't for any reason – just for the fun of it. We dragged old logs over from the forest and piled them into a triangle together. Sam got some white paint he found somewhere and tossed it all over. It used to glow at night. It was a laugh. I don't know why we ever did it. It went in the bushfire we had in '74. The fire jumped the creek, came up towards the house, burnt down the fences and the sheds and then it took our pyramid before the wind changed. Thirty yards, that was all. Last night I thought I saw it glowing out there,' she says, looking real strange. 'I could have sworn it was there. I was praying for Sam.'

'I always pray for him,' I say, 'but I don't know the words.'

Tegwyn makes a fart noise with her mouth. Mum looks at me kind of sad.

'You still pray for him, Henry?' Mum says. She looks hard at him like never before.

It's quiet for a while. Henry Warburton looks like he's got a splinter somewhere. And frightened. He's got frightened listening to us.

I eat the rest of my curry. It's nice and hot; makes me ears burn. Henry Warburton sits there looking at Mum real scared.

After, when we bring the sherry out for the Lord's Supper, Henry says he has to go to the toilet. Mum says it without him. 'Help us to be more than we are,' she prays. 'Help Henry.' We sit in the loungeroom by the fire. Mum sits with Dad's head on her lap. He lies across the sofa with a blanket. She rubs his face and looks at his wonky eyes and then looks at the fire a lot. Henry comes back in.

'I sometimes wonder if I haven't come to the end of my tether,' Mum says to no one exactly. 'Sometimes.'

I look up from the fire. So does Henry Warburton. Tegwyn is going to sleep on the floor with a pillow and blanket.

'Yes,' he says.

'What right have you got to agree?' she says, real quiet. 'You're not in my position.'

'I've got my own surviving to do.'

'It's not survival we worry about, Henry, it's healing.'

'Isn't it the same thing?'

'No. Healing is what you do for someone else. Survival is for yourself. You can eat people if you want to survive bad enough. Or you can die if you want to heal someone bad enough.'

'Well, you have been thinking, Alice.'

'Don't talk to me like that.'

'Death is a healing, too, you know.'

It's quiet for a long time. In the end I get up and go to my room. I check Barry and give him some sultanas from my pocket. Then I pray.

'This lizard is crook, God. I reckon you should make it better. I really do. What else can I say?'

In the morning I check on Barry and find him stiff under the wardrobe. I open the window and chuck him out.

Chapter Eighteen

'One week to Easter,' Henry Warburton says.

'More crap from you,' Tegwyn says.

'Tegwyn, please,' says Mum.

It's Sunday and raining and we're all stuck inside together. Henry Warburton goes on about Easter. How today is Palm Sunday when Jesus galloped in on the donkey and they all had leaves for him. After that he got arrested and the soldiers whipped him and put prickles in his hair and killed him by making two pieces of wood and sticking him to it with nails. When he died some bloke put him in a cave. Three days later he came back from the dead. People went beserk. Later he went into heaven. Then people talked a lot about it.

Tuesday it's the Passover. That's when God came over and people put blood on their door. When Jesus did the Lord's Supper, it was on the Passover. Think that's right. There's so much stuff to remember, I can't keep it all in me brain. Least there's a story to it which is better than school.

When it stops raining, I go out on the back verandah. Tegwyn comes out too.

'Do you really believe that garbage he tells you?' she says. She doesn't look at me; she looks out over the wet yard. Chooks fight for good pozzies in the roosts.

'Yeah. I reckon it's true.'

'Even though Henry Warburton's such a dickhead?'

'It's not him we believe in – it's, it's Jesus.'

'And you still think Warburton knows *mysterious* things?'

'Oh, yeah. Some things. He knew all our names and everything about Dad.' I look at her. There's a smile on her face. It's not nice.

'Do you think it's easier to believe because you're – you know – a bit . . . slow?' She grins and her teeth are pointy and aimed at me. 'Warburton's a bloody fake. He knew our names because he was skulkin' round the place for weeks. He asked people all about us. He saw us swimming. I was in the nick. Remember, buddy-boy?'

'That wasn't your fault, then.'

'Oh, come on, Stumblebum, wake up.'

'We went for a swim,' I say. 'You asked me to. I got you out of the shop that time. You –'

'Oh, don't be pathetic. I knew he was there. I knew what was going on. I didn't need to go with *you*.'

I can't stay. I go inside to my room and get under my pillow and just bawl and bawl. It's all horrible. I stuff the pillow in me mouth till it near makes me sick.

When I wake up it's dark. I can hear the hot water hissing in the pipes. I had this dream. I was here in the house and white birds were coming over, hundreds of them coming out of nowhere. They came around in a circle and then started to land in the trees. Pretty soon they filled the forest. Like snow. The forest was white and moving. And then it was over and here I am listening to the pipes.

I get up and go into the hallway. Henry Warburton's talking.

'. . . why I can't heal you, Sam. I'm unclean. I wake up at night with her smell on me, it's thick in the room. A succubus, Sam. That's what it's like. Bobo comes back to have me. It suffocates me, I tell you. I want her and I want to escape her. It makes me desire her and the thought of her makes me ill. Is it her? Or the other half of me? Is it the Powers? Is it my fault it's happening to me like this?

'I haven't told you something about her death, Sam. Oh, God, how can I say this? The reason I'm tainted, Sam, is because she died while we . . . were . . . while we. She died on me. Over me. I wonder if the bitch didn't do it on purpose, to mark me for life. She marked me with death, Sam. The same part of a woman that brings forth life. In the act that makes life. She died on me.

'I want to love. I do love. I want to love purely. I want that kind of love that heals, that soothes. I want to love properly. I want to *heal* you, Sam Flack. You will save me, Sam. Your healing will heal me. Or, Goddamn it, I'm lost.'

I go up into the loungeroom where Mum is sitting by the fire looking into it. I sit down next to her.

'Mum?'

'Hm?'

'Do you still love Dad?'

'Of course.'

'I thought maybe you loved Henry. You started to dress up.'

She puts a hand to her throat and there's tears coming in her eyes. 'Oh, Ort. I'm so lonely. A woman needs a man.'

'Dad's still a man.'

'I know now. I'm growing up, Ort. You can't see on the outside, but I am. Be patient.'

I really want to say 'I love you, Mum' but it sounds so crummy I can't do it.

'Are we supposed to put blood on our doors on Tuesday, do you think?' she says.

'I don't think so,' I say.

'Good. I didn't feel like doing something like that. It's barbaric. If only I was a smarter person. Maybe then I'd understand things.'

'Both of us must be a bit dumb, then.'

She looks at me and smiles.

I go out and look at the sky but it's blank; no stars, nothing.

Today is Thursday and tomorrow will be Good Friday. Mum said this hospital person came today and did tests on Dad and asked Mum all these questions about the colour of Dad's pee and how many times he went in a day and did he this or that. She said this girl poked him all over with her fingers and put a torch in his eye and shouted at him and hit him with a little hammer. She tore all the plaster off him – took his hair out. The woman went crook at Mum for not looking after him better. Mum is restless now. She walks around the house like there's ants in her pants.

'I just resent it, that's all,' she says, 'I resent it.'

Tegwyn and Henry Warburton are arguing again. They fight all the time in her room; he uses all the big words on her like *salvation* and *sanctification* and she yells at him and tells him to go stuff his head up Margaret's bum.

Later I come out after scrubbing potatoes for Mum, and I see Tegwyn throw the potful of tealeaves all on Henry Warburton, on his face, in his hair – everything. He picks her up and puts her over the rail of the steps and smacks her. Her dress is all up over her head and her knickers are black and he smacks her and smacks her until she screams and bawls.

After tea I go into the bathroom to brush my teeth to get out all the bits of meat and there's Henry Warburton bleeding into the sink. Blood's all coming out his nose and it runs all over his chin and into the white sink. He looks at me in the mirror.

'Not a word.'

I go out.

Before bed I go out and stand in the yard and look at that crazy light on our house. It just looks like it's sitting there waiting for a bus or something.

In the middle of the night I wake up. There's someone here in the room. Can feel it. I stay still, like a bit of firewood. I wait. No one moves.

'Who's there? Who is it?'

Down the hall I hear Grammar's voice: 'Is that you, Lil Pickering?'

I turn my bedside light on real quick. No one there. I get up and go down to Grammar's room. She's all up in a ball with the sheet on her head and the blankets all around.

'Is that you, Lil Pickering?'

'No, Gram, it's me, Ort.' I sit on the bed. 'Who do you hear, Grammar? Who came just then? I heard them. Who was it?'

'Pickering? Biscuits. Springtime? Mozart? Will you bring them? Am I ready? Will you come for me?'

Poor Grammar. Who? But I heard them. Someone has been here, you can feel it.

I go out into the hall and go down to Mum's room. She's in there crying. I go in.

'What's the matter?'

'Oh, Ort. I can't be expected to hold everything in.'

'The hospital person?'

'No, it's something else. The hospital girl was an excuse.'

'What, then?' I sit on the bed. Dad is snoring.

'I got a letter today. The wreckers want to know a few things. They're giving us early warning, they said.'

'What? What?'

'It looks like Henry didn't get the car in the proper way. It looks as though he's stolen it. Our car doesn't really belong to us. Henry lied.'

When's it gonna stop? God, when's it all gonna finish and leave us alone?

Chapter Nineteen

We're not eating today. Mum and me just can't. Nothing happens all day. It's Good Friday. There's bugger-all that's good about it. We do nothing all day, me and Mum, except in the morning we wash Dad. It's my idea to get him before Henry Warburton does. Tegwyn and him fight all day. The noise of it gets to you after a while.

At tea Mum says to Henry Warburton will he do something special for Easter tonight, but he says he's too busy, that something more important is calling him. He looks sick as a dog and that 'Nngth' is back real bad. Mum gives him and Tegwyn their tea with cold looks, and I take Dad's to him and she goes to Grammar.

'We're going to church tonight, Ort,' she says, real quiet in the hall. 'If you want to.'

'Not the one with all the greasy hair and grapejuice!'

'No, the big one. The Catholic one. I never thought of it before, but I have to do something. I have to.'

I shrug. 'Okay.'

We organize Tegwyn and Henry Warburton to look after the sick ones, and we get in the stolen 1958 FC Holden Special and drive in to Bankside.

Well! What a place. Right away we get in there we don't know what the hell's going on for a minute. There's candles all up the front and dark everywhere else and we go up the front so we can see. There's only a few people there. No one says one single word for a long time until this bloke with a dressing gown and a party hat comes down the aisle. Then there's stuff happening all over the place – people in white sheets, music coming flat-chat out of these pipes up the front and some bloke singing or talking like nothing you've ever heard before in your life. Scary, boy! This talking and singing going on and on with candles going out every now and then. It gets darker and darker. I can feel Mum grabbing me arm. Me fingers start throbbing. I don't know what's happening. No one talks to me or Mum – it all just happens. And all the time I'm looking up at this statue up on the wall, trying to figure out who it reminds me of. It's Jesus on the cross in the statue, I s'pose, but it reminds me of someone I know better.

More candles going out. Creepy singing. Mum is bawling now. That long hair, those wonky eyes, those holes in him – it looks like my Dad. That's who it is. Then it's real dark and I get Mum up and take her out and people go 'Ssh!' at us and I tell them up their bum and take Mum out to the car.

'I. Can't. Drive,' she sobs. 'Cant. Drive. State. I'm. God.'

So I put her in the back, get her to lie down on the seat, and I drive the stolen 1958 FC Holden Special all the way home. In one gear. I thought it would be easy, but it's not. The car goes all over the place. I knock down six fence posts and go into the storm gutter at the side of the road twice and get out again. Mum bawls in the back. I can hardly see out the windscreen. Rabbits run all over the road.

I keep it straight all the way down the drive, but I don't stop properly and I take a bit off the back shed. I get Mum inside and put her in bed with Dad and she cuddles up to him, still crying. Everything is dark. Me brain is going flat-chat and I can't keep still. I look in on Grammar. She's asleep. I look in on Tegwyn. I see the big lump in the bed. I see Henry Warburton's hairy arm. I see them in bed together and I go to my room and think.

I lie there thinking for a long time. I think about my Dad being a good man and him being smashed up for no reason. I think about

God and Jesus and Henry Warburton and his dreams and his false
eye. And I think about my sister Tegwyn who can't love us. And I
think about Grammar punching someone in the teeth with one
hand and playing beautiful music with the other . . .

In the night I wake up.
   'Who's there?'
   I turn the light on. Grammar is calling.
   I get up and go into the hall. I look in on Tegwyn and her and
him are biting each other and hitting each other, with his hairy
bum up and her making hate noises at him and the bed squealing.
   I go down to Grammar.
   'Coming for me. Waiting a long . . . old I am. Too old.'
   I go to sleep there.

Everyone is very quiet today. Henry Warburton works on the
stolen car. Tegwyn paints her nails on the verandah. Mum cooks,
quiet, not speaking. I see her hands shaking. The whole day goes
away like that. Except that I see things. Those canisters change all
day. The rubies and diamonds and things come and go all day.
Mum doesn't notice; like she's seeing something far inside herself;
birds look in the window. One flies against the glass and kills itself
and I bury it. The fire in the stove keeps going out. And I keep
lighting it. In the evening everyone stays in their rooms. I go to
sleep early, like I haven't been asleep all my life.

Chapter Twenty

In the morning I know. Mum is crying. I get up and do a check. My whole body is heavy, like I'm wrapped in a blanket. I can hardly walk. There's this mist, like me eyes've got something in them. Cloudy. Through all the holes and cracks in this old house, there's stuff coming in. It's like cloud but it's light. Coming in the cracks. Mum is in Grammar's room. She's half on the bed and Grammar is grey and all gone in the face and I know she's gone.

'She's dead,' Mum says, without looking up.

I feel sick and heavy, and all this light is pouring in like smoke and I go out into the hall again and open Tegwyn's door. The bed is empty. Even the blankets and sheets are gone. I open a cupboard. Empty. I go into the loungeroom and see all Henry Warburton's stuff gone and only his Bible on the sofa. Me heart is smashing around. The cloudy white light is coming in – I breathe it in; it's warm and it tastes good. Me head's nearly bursting. I go to the window. The car is gone. Big skid marks all over the drive. Birds shout in the trees. The smell of bush flowers comes in real strong. I can smell milk. I can smell the honey from the bees. The dying trees look strong and thick and all the colours come in the window like someone's pouring them in on us. A bell ringing from the forest – it makes the china rattle in the kitchen and it puts tingles up me back and makes me hair electric. Everywhere, in through all my looking places and the places I never even thought of – under the doors, up through the boards – that beautiful cloud creeps in. This house is filling with light and crazy music and suddenly I know what's going to happen and it's like the whole flaming world's suddenly making sense for a second and I run to the kitchen and grab the big bottle of SAFFLOWER OIL and back into the loungeroom and snatch up the big black Bible and burst into Mum's room and there's my Dad with these tears coming down his cheeks, pinpoints of light that hurt me eyes, tears like diamonds, I tell you. His eyes are open and they're on me and smiling as I come in shouting 'God! God! God!' His face is shining. I'm shaking all over. 'God! God! God!'

I get the lid off the bottle wading through the music, and the oil splashes all over him and Mum comes in laughing and the cloud fills the room till all I can see is his eyes burning white and I know that something, something here in this world is gonna break.

Tim Winton was born in 1960 and was educated in Perth and Albany, Australia. His first novel, *An Open Swimmer,* was the joint winner of the 1981 Australian/ Vogel Literary Award. He has been a full-time writer since 1982, and has had stories published in many Australian magazines. In 1983 he received a Writer's Fellowship from the Literature Board of the Australian Council. *Shallows,* his second novel, won the 1984 Miles Franklin Award in Australia. He lives in West Perth, Western Australia, with his wife, Denise, and their son, Jesse.

LILA, LILA

David Kern est serveur dans un bar branché. N'ayant pas de gros moyens financiers, il a l'habitude d'acheter ses meubles à bas prix chez un brocanteur. Un jour, il trouve dans le tiroir d'une vieille table le manuscrit d'un roman qu'un auteur aurait oublié là avant de se suicider. Peu après, David rencontre Marie, cliente du bar où il travaille et passionnée de littérature. Il en tombe follement amoureux et, dans l'espoir de l'émouvoir, il lui donne à lire le manuscrit qu'il a trouvé en se faisant passer pour son auteur. Marie est bouleversée par cette lecture. Elle trouve le livre si formidable qu'elle le fait parvenir à une maison d'édition qui décide de le publier. Le roman devient un best-seller...

David devrait être comblé, Marie n'a d'yeux que pour lui, et pourtant... Il va non seulement lui falloir endosser le costume de l'écrivain célèbre, se pliant aux séances de signature et aux dîners mondains, mais aussi vivre avec l'angoisse permanente d'être démasqué. Quant à Marie, l'aime-t-elle véritablement pour ce qu'il est ou pour ce qu'il représente ? Comment vit-on dans la peau d'un imposteur ?

Né en Suisse en 1948, publicitaire de formation, Martin Suter vit aujourd'hui à Ibiza. Il est l'auteur de plusieurs scénarios et tient deux chroniques hebdomadaires dans les journaux Weltwoche *et* Neue Zürcher Zeitung. *Il est l'auteur de quatre romans, dont* Small World, La Face cachée de la lune *et* Un ami parfait.

Martin Suter

LILA, LILA

ROMAN

Traduit de l'allemand
par Olivier Mannoni

Christian Bourgois éditeur

TEXTE INTÉGRAL

TITRE ORIGINAL
Lila, Lila

ÉDITEUR ORIGINAL
Diogenes Verlag AG, Zürich

© original : 2004 by Diogenes Verlag AG, Zurich

ISBN 2-02-066683-9
(ISBN 2-267-01725-3, 1ʳᵉ publication)

© Christian Bourgois éditeur, 2004, pour la traduction française

www.seuil.com

À Gretli.

Et ce Peter Landwei, c'était moi.

Il fit tourner le cylindre de l'Underwood noire jusqu'à ce que la dernière phrase apparaisse, s'alluma une cigarette et lut la page aux lignes serrées.

> *La pluie sourde tambourinait toujours sur les tuiles. Il ouvrit la fenêtre de la mansarde. Le crépitement se fit plus bruyant et plus aigu. Deux mètres en dessous de la corniche, l'eau de la gouttière disparaissait en gargouillant dans le tuyau d'évacuation. La rue trempée reflétait la faible lueur de l'unique réverbère de l'impasse. Devant l'immeuble d'en face était garée la fourgonnette à l'enseigne de la « Sellerie-tapisserie Maurer ». Derrière une vitrine portant la même enseigne, la lumière brillait comme chaque soir depuis que la femme de Maurer était morte. Et comme chaque soir, dans une chambre, au premier étage de la même maison, un homme chauve lisait, assis dans le faisceau lumineux d'un lampadaire. Aussi immobile qu'une poupée de cire. Les autres fenêtres étaient obscures, mis à part une lucarne près de la cheminée. Parfois, jadis,*

Peter s'était demandé qui habitait là-bas. Aujourd'hui, ça lui était égal. Autant que tout ce qui n'avait pas de rapport avec Sophie. Sophie que lui aussi désormais laissait de marbre.

Il ferma la fenêtre et prit une photographie encadrée sur le bureau. Sophie en maillot de bain. Elle avait tendu derrière elle une serviette-éponge des deux bras, comme si elle s'apprêtait à la poser sur ses épaules. Ses cheveux étaient trempés et brillants. Elle souriait.

C'était la seule photographie que Peter détenait de Sophie. Elle la lui avait offerte. Autrefois, la regarder lui donnait un pincement au cœur, parce qu'elle ne voulait pas lui dire qui l'avait prise. À présent, la photo lui serrait le cœur parce qu'il ne reverrait plus jamais Sophie.

Il sortit la photo du cadre et la glissa dans la poche intérieure de son lourd blouson de motard. Puis il éteignit la lumière et ferma la chambre. Il laissa la clef dans la serrure.

Dans l'escalier flottaient les odeurs d'oignons cuits à l'étuvée et de la cire que quelqu'un venait d'étaler sur le linoléum recouvrant les marches usées.

Une demi-heure plus tard, il avait atteint Rieten. La pluie n'avait pas diminué. L'écho des sombres façades déformait le bruit de moteur de sa Ducati.

À la sortie de la petite ville commençait la route nationale qui, un kilomètre de ligne droite plus loin, disparaissait dans le tunnel du Rotwand.

Peter passa la vitesse la plus élevée et fonça

à pleins gaz vers l'entrée du tunnel. Il avait été creusé à la dynamite dans une paroi rocheuse qui se dressait à la perpendiculaire au-dessus de la vallée, comme un mur. Le jour, quand la visibilité était bonne, on le distinguait à cinq cents mètres de distance, semblable à un trou de souris. En l'apercevant, les automobilistes levaient le pied malgré eux, comme s'ils craignaient de ne pas bien viser ce petit orifice.

Pourtant on ne pouvait pas manquer l'entrée du tunnel du Rotwand. Même la nuit.

Sauf si on le faisait exprès, comme Peter Landwei.

Et ce Peter Landwei, c'était moi.

Il tapa le chiffre *84* en bas de page, sortit la feuille de la machine et la déposa, page écrite retournée, sur les autres feuilles. Il rajusta la pile et la reposa sur son bureau, première page vers le haut.

On y lisait en grosses lettres : *SOPHIE, SOPHIE*. Et en dessous : *roman*. Et en dessous encore : *par Alfred Duster*.

Il ouvrit la fenêtre de la mansarde, écouta le roulement monotone de la pluie sur le toit de tuiles et observa l'homme immobile dans le faisceau lumineux de son réverbère.

Il ferma la fenêtre, prit son lourd blouson de motard dans l'armoire, le passa, éteignit la lumière et referma la porte de la chambre. Il laissa la clef dans la serrure.

Devant la maison, il démarra sa Ducati au kick, essuya de la main les gouttes sur la selle et s'y installa.

Lorsque le moteur mugit dans l'impasse, l'homme immobile leva un bref instant les yeux de son livre.

2

En temps normal, David était réveillé par l'odeur du déjeuner que préparait Mme Haag dans l'appartement voisin.

Mais ce jour-là, ce fut une brûlure à l'oreille droite qui l'arracha au sommeil. C'était tout lui : la moitié de sa génération portait des piercings, mais il suffisait que lui se fasse poser une minuscule boucle au lobe de l'oreille pour qu'il attrape une infection.

Il alla repêcher son bracelet-montre dans la caisse de vin vide qui lui servait de table de nuit. Il n'était même pas dix heures; il avait dormi à peine cinq heures.

David s'assit sur le bord de son lit. Le jour, que l'on distinguait derrière les rideaux trop courts, plongeait la chambre dans une lumière blafarde qui donnait aux meubles de seconde main – une table, des chaises, un fauteuil, des portemanteaux, une étagère – l'aspect d'une photo noir et blanc en trois dimensions. Les seules touches de couleur étaient les petites lampes rouges et vertes indiquant que sa chaîne hi-fi, son imprimante et son ordinateur étaient en veille.

Il passa un peignoir bleu clair délavé frappé des mots « Sauna Happy », ouvrit la porte de son appartement et sortit.

Les toilettes se trouvaient sur le palier. C'était désagréable, surtout en ce moment, à la saison froide, car elles n'étaient pas chauffées. Mais au moins, David était le seul à les utiliser. Pour des motifs insondables, le logement de Mme Haag avait des toilettes particulières.

Dans le miroir au-dessus du lavabo, il inspecta son oreille. Le point où elle était percée avait rougi et enflé. Il fut tenté d'enlever le bijou qui lui traversait le lobe. Mais dans ce cas, à ce qu'il avait entendu dire, le trou se refermerait.

Il rentra dans son appartement, remplit la cafetière et la posa sur le gaz. Puis il se doucha dans la cabine en aluminium et plexiglas opaque qu'un précédent locataire avait installée dans la cuisine, des années plus tôt.

Lorsqu'il sortit de la douche, la soupape de la cafetière crachait de l'eau, teintant la flamme de jaune. Il coupa le gaz, se sécha et remit son peignoir. Il prit une tasse dans l'évier, la lava et y versa du café. Dans le réfrigérateur se trouvait un pack de lait entamé. Il le renifla, en renversa un peu dans la tasse, la porta dans la chambre, la posa sur la table de chevet, alluma sa chaîne et se glissa de nouveau sous la couverture. Prendre son café au lit était un luxe auquel David Kern n'aimait pas renoncer.

La radio était calée sur une station qui diffusait toute la journée de la musique des Tropiques. Un sacré contraste avec le climat local : températures autour de zéro, une épaisse couche de nuages qui retombait tantôt en bruine, tantôt en neige. Les jours commençaient lorsque David dormait encore profondément, et s'étaient le plus souvent déjà achevés lorsqu'il quittait l'immeuble.

Il but son café à petites gorgées et se fit du souci pour son oreille. Peut-être devrait-il retourner à la

Winning Gold

Lorna Schultz Nicholson

James Lorimer & Company, Ltd., Publishers
Toronto

James Lorimer & Company Ltd. acknowledges the support of the Ontario Arts Council. We acknowledge the support of the Government of Canada through the Book Publishing Industry Development Program (BPIDP) for our publishing activities. We acknowledge the support of the Canada Council for the Arts for our publishing program. We acknowledge the assistance of the OMDC Book Fund, and initiative of Ontario Media Development Corporation.

Canada

The Canada Council | Le Conseil des Arts
for the Arts | du Canada

ONTARIO ARTS COUNCIL
CONSEIL DES ARTS DE L'ONTARIO

Cover design: Meredith Bangay

Library and Archives Canada Cataloguing in Publication

Schultz Nicholson, Lorna
    Winning gold : Canada's incredible 2002 Olympic victory in women's hockey / Lorna Schultz Nicholson.

Includes index.
ISBN 978-1-55277-472-4 (pbk.).—ISBN 978-1-55277-473-1 (bound)

    1. Women hockey players—Canada—Juvenile literature. 2. Winter Olympic Games (19th : 2002 : Salt Lake City, Utah)—Juvenile literature. 3. Hockey—Canada—History—21st century—Juvenile literature. I. Title.

GV848.6.W65S385 2009   j796.962'66   C2009-906863-X

James Lorimer & Company Ltd., Publishers
317 Adelaide Street West,
Suite #1002
Toronto, ON
M5V 1P9
www.lorimer.ca

Distributed in the U.S. by:
Orca Book Publishers
P.O. Box 468
Custer, WA USA
98240-0468

Printed and bound in Canada.

Manufactured by Webcom in Toronto, Ontario, Canada in November 2009.
Job # 364662

To the women of the 2002 O
Team, for believing! Canada is

Contents

Prologue

The January day was dark, damp, and overcast. Cassie Campbell and Vicky Sunohara walked in the misty rain along the Vancouver seawall with Bob Nicholson, President of Hockey Canada. He had flown in to meet with the captains to discuss what was wrong with the Canadian Women's National Hockey Team. *Why had they lost seven games in a row to the USA?* he wanted to know.

Maybe the team needs some changes, thought Bob.

At the 1998 Olympic Games in Nagano, Japan, Canada had lost in the gold-medal game to the USA. Everyone had expected the women to win. The loss had been a huge upset for the team, Hockey Canada, and Canadian fans. Now, four years later, no one wanted another silver medal. Gold was expected in the 2002 Winter Olympics in Salt Lake City.

Cassie and Vicky told Bob that the pre-Olympic losing streak was the players' fault, and not the fault of the coaches. Earlier in the day, Bob had met with the assistant captain of the team, Hayley Wickenheiser. He had met with her separately to get true reactions. She had told him the exact same thing.

The players needed to pull it together. Team Canada had a lot of experienced players. But for some reason, they were struggling. The breaks just never seemed to come their way. They needed a win.

The team was in Vancouver because they had one last game to play against the USA. The eighth pre-Olympic game would be held at the state-of-the-art General Motors Place the next day. After seven losses, Bob had concerns about the team. He tried to stay positive: If they won in Vancouver, they would head into the Olympic Games with at least one win. *That would certainly help*, he thought.

After the walk, Bob decided to stay to watch Game 8 in the pre-Olympic set. He would also be going to the Olympic Games, which began the next month in Salt Lake City, Utah, USA. There, he knew, Canadians would accept nothing less than their women's team bringing home the gold medal.

1 Final Faceoff

On Tuesday, January 8, 2002, Danièle Sauvageau addressed her team in the dressing room at General Motors Place in Vancouver. The media had called the game they were about to play the "Final Faceoff." The coach of the Canadian Women's Olympic Team didn't have a lot to say. She'd had her players practise the power play over and over again. She'd made them train hard. Sometimes the workouts she gave them were as hard as the workouts she'd had to do herself to become an RCMP officer. She'd even taken them to an army base that summer. There, she had them do some of the same drills the Canadian army had to do, running obstacle courses and climbing over cement walls.

Coach Danièle told them their lines. She talked about a few strategies they'd been working on in practice. The power play was important. And so was the penalty kill. The US team was known for their power play.

Over six thousand fans had come to watch the women play. Many were dressed in Team Canada jerseys and waved the Maple Leaf. They were very vocal. The players knew the game was being nationally televised. People from all across Canada would be hoping for a win.

Cameras snapped as the players stepped onto the ice.

With total confidence, Kim St. Pierre, starting goalie for that night's game, took her place in net. She shuffled back and forth in the crease. Today she had been given the green light to be goaltender for Canada. But both Kim and goalie Sami Jo Small wanted to earn the coveted spot of starting goaltender. The decision as to who would be the starting goalie for the Olympic tournament had not yet been decided.

When the whistle blew, the players lined up at centre ice. With the drop of the puck, the fast pace began. The Canadians started off strong and were out-shooting the USA. But then Canadian forward Lori Dupuis took a charging penalty. The clock read 3:48. The USA was on the power play.

The USA gained possession and immediately cycled the puck in the Canadian zone. Kim followed each play, moving from side to side in her net.

Shot after shot, Kim made saves. The Canadians managed to clear the puck out of their zone a couple of times, but the USA came right back in.

Then a shot came from the blue line. It was a hard one. The puck flew straight to the back of the net. The red light went on. Goal for the USA.

For the rest of the period, Coach Danièle kept a close eye on Kim from the bench. Kim had made two unbelievable saves in that first period. One was a booming shot from the point. The other was a glove-hand save on a shot that came from the slot. But was she playing well enough to be the starting goalie in Salt Lake City?

At the end of the first period, the Canadians were still down 1–0, even though they had outshot the USA 7–3.

The Canadians came back on the ice in the second period fired up. They were

Colleen Sostorics looking for a pass in pre-Olympic play.

only down one goal. At 12:43 in the second period, the Canadians' hopes soared. Forward Caroline Ouellette picked up the puck and passed it to Cassie. Cassie passed it to Hayley. Hayley fired the puck, sinking it to the back of the net. The crowd roared. The Canadians were on the scoreboard!

The score was still 1–1 when the buzzer announced the end of the second period. The Canadians had outshot the USA in the second period and were leading shots on goal by 21–11.

Just 1:18 into the third period, forward Jennifer Botterill rushed in to forecheck the USA defense. She managed to steal the puck behind the American net. With a quick wrist shot, she bounced the puck off the American goaltender and into the net. When the red light flashed, the team went crazy. Jennifer's unassisted goal had given the Canadians the lead for the first time in the game. Now they just had to hang on to it.

The Canadians continued to battle. They shot and shot at the USA goalie but she made save after save.

Then at 13:13 the USA somehow slipped one past Kim.

Everyone looked at the clock. The score was tied at 2–2. At the bench, the Canadians told each other they could still win. So far they'd outplayed the USA. All they had to do was keep shooting and put another one in the net. They lined up at the faceoff. The puck dropped. They battled.

Just over one minute later, the USA blasted a shot towards Kim. When it hit the back of the net, the Canadian players were stunned.

The Canadian women all looked up at the clock: 14:31. They had over five minutes to score and tie the game.

Although they worked hard and outshot the USA, the goal they needed never happened. When the buzzer went to end the game, the Canadian team had lost their eighth straight game to the USA by a score of 3–2. But they had outplayed their opponents. How could they have lost again? This was not the record they wanted heading into the Olympic Games.

Eight-and-Uh-oh!

Game 1 Oct. 20, 2001, in Salt Lake City:
 USA 4, Can 1

Game 2 Oct. 23, 2001, in San Jose:
 USA 4, Can 1

Game 3 Nov. 27, 2001, in Ottawa:
 USA 5, Can 2

Game 4 Nov. 28, 2001, in Montreal:
 USA 4, Can 3

Game 5 Nov. 30, 2001, in Hamilton:
 USA 1, Can 0

Game 6 Jan. 5, 2002, in Chicago:
 USA 3, Can 1

Game 7 Jan. 6, 2002, in Detroit:
 USA 7, Can 3

Game 8 Jan. 8, 2002, in Vancouver:
 USA 3, Can 2

2 Talking it Through

The Canadian women silently filed into the dressing room after the game. One by one they sat on the bench and leaned back against the concrete wall. No one attempted to undress and get out of their sweat-soaked equipment. The door leading to the lobby remained locked. They needed time to absorb what had happened, and they didn't want anyone in the room, not even the coaches.

After five minutes, some of the players

broke the silence with comments about the game, saying that if they kept trying, they would get better. But Hayley was still stinging from the loss and she just couldn't listen. She didn't want to fluff this over. So instead, she raised her voice to talk openly about her frustration. Upon hearing how upset Hayley was, many of the players became emotional.

As captain, Cassie realized she needed to control what was going on. "Hayley has brought up some good points," she said. "We need to talk this through."

Cassie's words were like a dam breaking. They gave the players the okay to vent. Some yelled, some whispered, others just talked. Many cried.

For more than forty-five minutes, they remained in the dressing room, in their equipment, discussing what had gone wrong. They hashed over their losses. They talked through the problems, and they

Team Captains

There were three team captains on the women's hockey team. The captain was Cassie Campbell, who is the most captained player in the history of hockey in Canada. Assistant Captain Vicky Sunohara played in the first ever Women's World Hockey Championships in 1990 in Ottawa, Ontario. That was the year the Canadian Women's Hockey Team wore pink and white jerseys! Assistant Captain Hayley Wickenheiser was playing in her third Olympic Games in 2002. Hayley had played hockey in the 1998 Winter Olympics and she had also played on the Canadian Softball Team in the 2000 Summer Olympics.

talked about what they needed to do to get better.

Then the team decided that they still believed they could win at the Olympics. They would have to put the eight losses behind them. Gold was still within reach.

The time they spent in the dressing

*Cassie Campbell was the captain of the 2002
Women's Olympic Hockey Team.*

room that night was the turning point for
the Canadian Women's Olympic Hockey
Team. They decided then and there how

much they wanted to win gold. Some of the women had played on the 1998 Olympic team. They knew what it felt like to come home with silver.

When they had finished, Cassie said, "What a story this will be."

While the players were inside the dressing room, André Brin, Manager of Media Relations for Hockey Canada, had reporters line up outside. Many of the reporters were on deadlines and had to get their stories to press.

Coach Danièle had also stayed outside the dressing room. The players needed to work this out for themselves. She had already told them they had practice the next day back in Calgary — a morning practice. She wasn't going to give them any rest. Last she had heard she was still coach, so she eased the anxieties of the deadline-driven reporters pacing in the hallway by answering questions.

"Right now we have all the big pieces, and I'm going to search for the little thing [to make a difference]," Danièle said. "We're going to compete. Battle to the end. You can't push a button and say, 'Fifth floor, please.' In order to get to the top you've got to climb the stairs one by one."

When the players finally started filing out of the dressing room, there was a calm surrounding them.

Jennifer stopped to talk to a reporter from the *Vancouver Sun*. "It's easy to understand how from the outside you can look at the record and be very concerned. However, within the team we still feel extremely confident in knowing we're going to come together and peak at the right time with our performance at the Olympics."

Goaltender Sami Jo Small was next on the *Sun* reporter's hit list. From the bench, she'd had a front-row seat for the game. "It does matter that we've lost ... don't get me wrong," she said. "But there is really only one game that really matters and that's February 21 [the Olympic gold-medal final]."

Across the country many doubted that the Canadian Women's Hockey Team could win an Olympic gold medal. Eight losses were just too much to come back from. Under a headline that read, "Canadian Women confident of managing miracle on ice," a *Calgary Herald* sports reporter wrote: "The losses have been piling up like dirty laundry in the bottom of a closet. They're up to eight stinkin' defeats and counting now."

But the players had decided that night that they could still win. They still believed. Would that be enough?

3 Tough Choices

The team arrived back in Calgary after midnight. They were staying in dorms across the street from the Father David Bauer arena in Calgary, where they trained.

The next morning, a number of players showed up to practice a few minutes late. When they got there, the door was locked. Coach Danièle had locked it. Any player who wasn't there at the exact time she told them to be there, wouldn't be practising with the team.

Only eight players out of twenty-one ended up practising that morning.

While some of the players were standing outside, Hockey Canada personnel were inside their offices at the arena discussing the team.

Bob Nicholson's phone had rung all night with calls from the media, and was still ringing that morning. The media's questions were rapid and cutting: What was wrong with the women's program? What did he think about the eight losses in a row? What plans did he have for the team now? Was he going to make any changes?

The team had played well. They had lost, but they had definitely stepped up their game. He had decided he wasn't going to make any changes to the coaching staff.

Bob wasn't the only one thinking about changes. For weeks, Danièle had been in discussions with her three assistant coaches, Wally Kozak, Melody Davidson, and Karen Hughes. They talked constantly about what they could do to make the team better and get them on the winning path. They had gone through each player and discussed her role on the team.

After a long talk, the coaches were ready to make some roster changes.

They met with veteran forward Nancy Drolet in private and told her she was cut from the team. Cherie Piper would be taking Nancy's spot.

Hockey Canada sent out a press release January 14. It read: "Canada's National Women's Team Adjusts Roster for Salt Lake City."

The press release had the media buzzing. The *Calgary Herald* wanted to write about this shake-up. They talked to Danièle. She said, "I was hired to put the best team on the ice, and this is what we thought was the best decision, and we

The 2002 Canadian Women's Hockey Team and the Hockey Canada management team at the Father David Bauer arena prior to leaving for Salt Lake City.

made it. It was very well thought out and not something we decided overnight. It has been going on for weeks and months."

Some of the players didn't take the announcement well. Many felt insecure about their position on the team. If Nancy could be let go, then who was next? And many on the team were going to miss Nancy. She had been a national team

The Nancy Drolet Appeal

On January 17, 2002, Nancy Drolet registered an appeal to get back on the team so she could play in the Salt Lake City Olympics. Nancy's appeal made national headlines and became a heated issue. On January 27, 2002, she lost her appeal.

member and a veteran player and was well liked.

At the next practice after the announcement, Cherie Piper arrived ready to take her new place on the team.

Cherie had been working hard, moving up the hockey ladder. She'd been disappointed to have been left off the Olympic roster in November, but had continued training hard with the team. She knew this was her big chance.

On February 6, the final members of the Women's Olympic Team boarded the plane for Salt Lake City.

4 Quote du Jour

Arriving in Salt Lake City, the team was taken to the Olympic Village to get settled in their rooms. After they unpacked their bags, they were told to meet so they could all get their accreditation. They lined up and got their photos taken, then the photos were put on a piece of paper and laminated. It was almost like getting a passport. And they had to wear this around their necks at all times. If they didn't, they wouldn't get into the Olympic Village, where athletes from all over the world, from every sport, were housed for their duration at the Olympics.

The Olympic Flame burns brightly during the Opening Ceremonies.

Once every player had their accreditation slung around their necks, it was
time to get ready for practice. In five days
they would step on the ice to play their
opening game in the 2002 Winter
Olympics.

Canada had been put in a round-robin
pool with Kazakhstan, Russia, and Sweden.
Their first game was against Kazakhstan.
The other round-robin pool was made up
of teams from Finland, China, Germany,
and Canada's powerful rival — the USA.
The winner from one pool would play the
second-place winner from the other pool
in the semi-final games. Then the winners
of the semi-finals would play each other
for the gold-medal game. The winner took
gold; the loser, silver.

The two teams that lost in the semi-
finals would battle each other in the
bronze-medal game.

The Olympic Games started with a

spectacular Opening Ceremonies. Wearing red leather Roots coats, striped scarves, and tam-style hats, the Canadian Women's team lined up at the athletes' entrance with the rest of the Canadian Olympians.

Rumours about security for that night had filtered through the Olympic Village. Just five months before, on September 11, 2001, the World Trade Center in New York City had been attacked by terrorists. Because of 9/11, the Americans had extra security in place. There were snipers on rooftops. Helicopters flew overhead.

At the entrance, the Canadians listened to the President of the United States, George W. Bush, speak. They heard the Mormon Tabernacle Choir sing. Then the crowd hushed as a flag from the World Trade Center was raised. It was an emotional moment for everyone. A beautiful display of fireworks then began as the athletes entered. Speed skater Catriona

Le May Doan carried the Canadian flag. The Canadian group included 157 members, the fourth-largest at the Games.

The team's spirit was good following the Opening Ceremonies. For two days the Canadian Women's Hockey Team practised and did dry-land workouts. Getting out of Canada and into the Village had given them time to concentrate.

As a team, they decided that for motivation they would put together groups to come up with a *quote du jour* for each game. The quotes were meant to inspire their teammates to play the best they could. The team had to keep believing that they could win the gold. In the first group were Jennifer, forward Tammy Lee Shewchuk, forward Kelly Béchard, and Sami Jo.

The day of the game, the players stood before the rest of the team in the dressing room and said in unison, "Today's game

Team Roster

Goaltenders: Charline Labonté #32, Sami Jo Small #1, Kim St. Pierre #33

Defense: Thérèse Brisson #6, Isabelle Chartrand #73, Geraldine Heaney #91, Becky Kellar #4, Cheryl Pounder #11, Colleen Sostorics # 5

Forwards: Dana Antal #23, Kelly Béchard #24, Jennifer Botterill #17, Cassie Campbell #77, Lori Dupuis #12, Danielle Goyette #15, Jayna Hefford #16, Caroline Ouellette #13, Cherie Piper #7, Tammy Lee Shewchuk #25, Vicky Sunohara #61, Hayley Wickenheiser #22

will set the tone for the rest of the tournament. Only we can determine the message we send — let's make it one of no regrets."

After the quote, the players proudly slipped their jerseys over their heads. On the front of each jersey was Canada's heritage patch. This was the same patch that had been on the jerseys that the men's team had worn in the 1952 Olympics, the last time Canada had won gold in hockey at the Games. The women were the first

Vicky Sunohara wearing the Canadian heritage jersey. Notice the Maple Leaf on the front.

Canadian team in fifty years to wear the patch.

Coach Danièle had been waffling over who should go in net. Picking the starting goalie for the Olympics would be difficult. Goaltenders Kim and Sami Jo had been together for years on the National Team. Charline Labonté was the third goalie, but she wouldn't dress unless Sami Jo or Kim got injured. Whichever goalie was chosen for a game understood she was the lucky one. Sometimes that decision wasn't made until the last moment.

Kim had even been questioned by reporters about the issue. She had told them, "This is our fourth year together and we're used to it. Every year it's the same story and we're not really disturbed by who will be number 1 and who will be number 2."

Fortunately for her, Kim was named the starting goalie for the game.

Coach Danièle took her place on the bench. The kind of game they had to play today would be difficult. Kazakhstan was no match for her team. But Canada would have to play their best anyway. Games where one team was definitely better than the other team were hard because they could create bad habits like sloppy passes and lazy skating. They had to stay sharp.

5 Opening Game

When the whistle shrilled to start the game, the Canadians lined up at centre ice. The puck dropped, and bounced. And it seemed to keep bouncing. Passes missed sticks and the Canadian players seemed unsettled. At 2:30 in the first period, Kazakhstan took a holding penalty. Canada was to go on the power play.

Coach Danièle put out her first power-play line. They had practised and practised the power play. It took only three seconds for Hayley to rifle off a hard shot that sunk to the back of the net. The Canadians were on the scoreboard.

Although the play started at centre ice, it didn't take long to move back in the Kazakhstan end. The Canadians controlled the play and kept shooting on the goalie, but none of their shots made the red light go on. The Kazakhstan goalie was sharp and kept plucking the puck out of mid-air.

Then at 8:45, forward Cherie Piper smacked the rebound off a shot by linemate Dana Antal into the back of the net. Goal! The players hugged.

.Less than one minute later, at 9:20, Canada was back on the power play. They passed the puck around but had trouble finding the net. The clock ticked down. Coach Danièle frowned. This wasn't the power play they'd practised. Then, with just eleven seconds left on the power play, defense Colleen Sostorics passed the puck

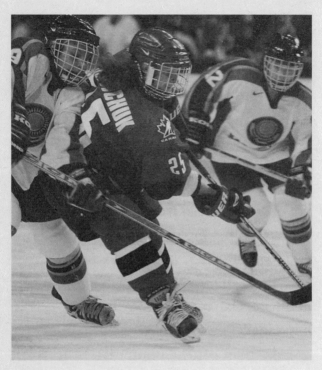

Tammy Lee Shewchuk breaking past a Kazakhstan player in the women's first Olympic Game.

to Cherie, who was hovering around in the slot. Cherie connected and fired the puck, but the Kazakhstan goalie dished out a rebound. Forward Vicky Sunohara swooped in for the rebound and scored Canada's third goal.

At the end of the first period, the score was 3–0 Canada.

The Canadian players talked about what they could do better. They were up 3–0, but they hadn't played great hockey. Their passes had been terrible.

Three minutes into the second period, Kazakhstan took another penalty and Canada was again on the power play. This time the puck moved from Colleen to forward Danielle Goyette to her linemate Tammy Lee Shewchuk, who scored her first goal of the game.

When Canada went into yet another power play, just five minutes before the end of the second period, forward Hayley Wickenheiser found the puck on her stick by fighting hard. She zipped towards the net. Firing the puck, she scored her second goal of the night. The assist went to Danielle.

Goalie Goods

• Kim St. Pierre is from Quebec. In 2001, at the World Championships, she was named top goaltender. Kim also played on the Quebec provincial softball team as a shortstop.

• Sami Jo Small made the 1998 Olympic team as third goalie. She didn't see any ice time. Sami Jo was also a really good discus and javelin thrower.

• Charline Labonté was the youngest player on the roster and had just made her debut on the National Team in 2001. Her first game was a shutout.

So far, Canada had scored four of their five goals on the power play. This pleased Coach Danièle, who had made them work on the power play over and over.

One more power-play goal was scored in the third period by Danielle on a pass from Hayley. The last goal of the game was scored by Vicky on yet another rebound from a shot by forward Jayna Hefford.

The shots were 66–11. When Kim took off her mask, she barely had sweat rolling down her face. Meanwhile the Kazakhstan goalie was exhausted. She'd made fifty-nine saves!

Even with a 7–0 victory, the Canadian team was not happy.

Defense Thérèse Brisson told a *Toronto Star* reporter, "It was shinny hockey, and we pretty much played that way. That was not great for us. In the first period, we were pretty much terrible."

Jennifer was a little more positive. "The USA is in the back of our minds, but we need to focus on each opponent."

Up in western Canada, a *Calgary Sun* reporter wrote, "Building toward the final against Team USA, Canada didn't exactly look like a well-oiled machine."

Another paper titled their article, "Seven Goals Not Enough."

The Canadian women had won one game and that meant they were one step closer to winning Olympic gold.

But the coaching staff and the players knew for this to come true they had a lot of work ahead of them.

6 Canada vs. Russia

The Canadian women had a day off between games to practise and regroup. During their down time, they gathered in the Olympic Village athletes' lounge to watch the other sports on television. There was huge controversy, too. In pairs figure skating, the Canadian team of Jamie Salé and David Pelletier had just lost the gold medal to the Russian pair. It was the talk of the Women's Hockey Team. They had all watched the event on television and were outraged by the judges' decision. And their team was playing the Russian hockey team next.

The Canadian Women's Hockey Team promised their skating friends a little payback. Vicky even said to a *Toronto Star* reporter, "We'll get them back for Jamie and David."

Cassie wrote up a note for her team and called it Captain's Corner. "*The definition of courage in the Defining Dictionary of the Living Russian language is 'Quiet Bravery, presence of mind in trouble or danger.'*" As a follow-up, in her own words, she wrote, "*How appropriate. Let's show the Russians our definition of courage and win it for David and Jamie!*"

As the team boarded the bus, ready to head to the arena, the players understood that they had to treat each game as important. They were a better team than Russia and would probably win. But in a tournament like the Olympics, a team had to get better every game. The tournament would only get tougher and tougher.

Before the game, Cherie, Caroline, Dana, and Kim got up and said their *quote du jour:* "So many people believe in you. Make sure you're one of them."

But when the puck dropped, the Canadians once again looked a little unsettled. The coaches thought the team looked as if they were playing down to the level of their opponents. The Russians were playing stubborn hockey and not giving Canada chances to score.

Halfway through the first period, the game remained scoreless. Finally, at 11:37, Hayley picked up the puck off the faceoff, powered to the net, and scored! The referee recorded it as an unassisted goal. Canada was on the scoreboard.

It was almost seven minutes later when Hayley passed the puck down along the boards. Danielle freed it and peppered a shot from the slot. Canada went to the dressing room with a 2–0 lead.

Just thirty-one seconds into the second period, Caroline took a pass from defense Geraldine Heaney and sent the puck over to Dana. Dana ripped off a quick shot to give Canada a 3–0 lead. Nine minutes later, Caroline, who was at the side of the net with the puck, looked up. She saw Cherie positioned perfectly in the slot. She passed the puck over, and Cherie one-timed it. The goal gave Canada a 4–0 lead.

A deflected goal started off the scoring seven minutes into the third period. Vicky sent off a high shot and Jennifer, hanging around the front of the net, deflected it past the Russian goalie. It was Canada's first power-play goal of the game.

Canada scored twice more before the end of the period. Their sixth goal was deflected two times before defense Isabelle

Caroline Ouellette ready to take a shot in Canada's game against Russia.

Chartrand — who was playing in her first Olympics — sunk it into the back of the net.

Fast Forwards Facts

• Dana Antal was born in Saskatchewan. In the 1997–98 season, Dana played in the National Swiss League.

• Kelly Béchard is from Sedley, Saskatchewan. Kelly won the Saskatchewan Provincial Badminton Championships in girls' doubles while in high school.

• Caroline Ouellette graduated from the National Police Academy in Quebec in the fall of 2000.

• Tammy Lee Shewchuk is a Harvard graduate. On January 7, 2001, she became the NCAA all-time leading scorer for women's hockey by scoring her 258th goal.

The final goal — number seven — saw Danielle weaving her way through the crowd and zinging a shot from the slot.

The score was 7–0 for Canada. Canada had outshot the Russians 60–6.

Sami Jo had been in net for Canada. The coaches were still trying to figure out who their starting goalie would be for the semi-finals and finals. Sami Jo had only had to stop six shots. The action she had seen was in the last twenty seconds when the Russians had put the pressure on. For those twenty seconds, Sami Jo had worked hard to keep her shutout.

After the game, Sami Jo met with a reporter from the *Winnipeg Free Press*. Winnipeg was her hometown. She said, "As a goaltender, yeah, it's one shot every ten minutes; but I don't really see it that way. It's an Olympic game, and I get to watch these girls score some goals and make some pretty plays. I mean, you never get bored out there."

Although the win was sweet, the Canadians couldn't rest. They had to stay motivated and keep up their intensity.

The *Toronto Star* summed it up by saying, "As impressive as 14 goals in two shutout games may sound, the Canadians still don't look sharp."

The women knew, too, that they had to step it up if they wanted to beat the Finns and the Americans.

7 Poetry in Motion

The energy in the Olympic Village made the women eager to play again. One more game would put them closer to playing in the gold-medal game. In the Village, they met athletes from different sports, and some of their National Hockey League heroes. The Canadian Men's Team was full of NHL stars. Also staying at the Olympic Village was men's team captain Mario Lemieux. The general manager of their team was hockey legend Wayne Gretzky.

It came as a huge shock to everyone when the Canadian Men's Team lost to Sweden 5–2 in their first game. This had not gone over very well with the Canadian media. The women talked about how their next game was against Sweden. They wanted to win. They wanted revenge for the men's loss. This would be the women's last game of their round-robin pool.

The *quote du jour* grouping for that game was a line that played hard together: Vicky, Lori, and Jayna. When they met to come up with a quote, they started laughing about all the fun they'd had over the year. Their talk reflected back on the entire season. It started in May when the team had gotten together to train. Vicky decided that their memories needed to be put into a poem.

When they finished, they printed it for everyone to read.

Before the game, Vicky, Lori, and Jayna recited the poem out loud. The entire team cheered when they came to the last two verses:

> *The challenge is ahead of us*
> *To beat the Swedes and Finns*
> *To play consistent hockey*
> *And do 20 second spins*
>
> *The moral of the story*
> *Is easy to define*
> *We've worked too hard this year*
> *To end up 0 and 9.*

Then the three women also shared a quote that they had found by French poet Paul Valery: "The best way to make your dreams come true is to wake up."

In no time at all the ice was ready. The Canadians filed out of their dressing room for the start of the third and final game of their round robin.

The period started off slow and Canada

went ten minutes without a goal. Finally, at 10:26, Jennifer took a pass from Tammy at Sweden's blue line and managed to stickhandle her way around a Swedish player on right wing. With a clear path to the net, she cut across the front of the crease and shoved the puck in on the far side of the net. The Swedish goalie didn't know what hit her. She didn't even have time to shuffle across to cover her net.

Although the Canadians hammered off nineteen shots in the first period, Jennifer's was the only goal.

Cherie opened up the scoring just four minutes into the second period by batting at a bouncing puck. Then Jennifer scored her second goal by deflecting a long shot from Geraldine at the point on a power play. Then it was Hayley's turn to score on a pass from Cassie. Hayley moved in close and shot the puck waist high. The last goal of the period was scored by Cassie as she steered the puck into the net on a pass from Danielle, who was behind the net.

The Canadians decided to turn up the heat.

In the third period, they were relentless. They had opened the scoring gates. They put in six goals from six different players. Goals were scored by Caroline, Jayna, Lori, Vicky, Dana, and Isabelle. All in all, ten players scored and the Canadians ended up beating the Swedes 11–0. Jennifer was the only one to score more than one goal. Jayna recorded four points with one goal and three assists, and Jennifer picked up three points. She added one assist to her two goals.

In net, Kim stopped all twenty-two shots that came her way. The shots on net were 70–22 for Canada.

In the *Winnipeg Free Press*, the headline read, "Different story as Women Play. This Canada–Sweden hockey game was all about Canada." The *Toronto Star* wrote, "Revenge: How Swede it is," and the *Calgary Sun* wrote, "Ladies get Swede Revenge."

Meanwhile, the Canadian women knew that, while it was nice that they had beaten the Swedes in such a one-sided game to get revenge for the men's team, they had a tough semi-final ahead of them.

Canada had finished first in their round-robin pool with a 3–0 record. But so had the USA. As expected, they had also won all three of their round-robin games.

The stage was set. Canada was to play Finland in the semi-final match up. The USA would meet up with Sweden for their semi-final.

But Finland would be no pushover. At the IIHF 2001 World Championships, they had taken a very young team. For this Olympics, they had brought back a lot of veteran players.

Vicky summed it up when she talked to the *Globe and Mail*, "I really think they [the Finns] came here with the idea that they can upset us or the USA."

8 Finns Fight to the Finish

A win in the semi-final game would take the Canadian Women's Hockey Team to the gold-medal final. A loss would take them to the bronze-medal game. They had to win. They had to have one more chance to play the USA.

Cheryl Pounder, Colleen, Becky Kellar, and Isabelle were in charge of the *quote du jour*. All of them played defense. The quote they came up with for the game was by American civil rights activist Martin

Luther King Jr.: "The ultimate measure of a person is not where they stand in moments of comfort and convenience, but where they stand in times of challenge and adversity."

From the first puck drop, it was clear to the Canadians that Finland had come to play and win. But really, that was no surprise to the Canadian team.

Just four minutes and two seconds into the game, Canada was given a power play opportunity. They shot and shot but the Finnish goalie stood-on-her-head and made save after save.

With just four seconds left on the clock in the power play, Thérèse blasted a slapshot from the point. The puck sunk to the back of the net.

At the 8:10 mark, Hayley picked up the puck and, on a breakaway, nipped it between the pads of the Finnish goalie.

For the rest of the period it looked as if

Canada would go to the dressing room with a 2–0 lead. Was this going to be another shutout game for the Canadians? Kim was in net and hadn't seen a lot of shots.

The clock read 19:35. The period would end in just twenty-five seconds. But then one of the Finnish players picked up the puck and made a spectacular move. Kim tried to make the save, but the puck settled in the back of the net.

The buzzer sounded, and the Canadians headed to the dressing room with a 2–1 lead.

The mood between periods was positive and calm. The Canadians were still up. They could easily beat the Finns.

They headed out for the second period sure of a success.

But something wasn't quite clicking for the Canadians. They were making some defensive errors and giving the puck away.

At 2:56, just short of three minutes into the period, the Finns popped the puck by Kim.

Not even one minute later, the Finns scored again. The Canadian players looked at each other. How had this happened? Somehow, the Canadians had let the Finns score two unanswered goals to take the lead.

In the stands, the Canadian fans were on the edge of their seats. Would this be another final faceoff game?

At that moment, the Canadians decided to put the pressure on. They peppered the Finnish goalie with shot after shot. But shot after shot, she made the saves. Her acrobatic moves stunned the crowd. Were the Finns going to pull the biggest upset in the history of women's hockey? Were they going to beat Canada to advance to the gold-medal game?

No other goals were scored in the

second period. The buzzer went and the Canadians went to their dressing room down by a goal.

The crowd murmured in the stands.

Between periods, the media barraged Hockey Canada President Bob Nicholson.

"What's happening to women's hockey?"

"Why are they losing?"

"Will you have to make changes to your women's program?"

He replied to the media with the comment: "The last I heard there were three periods to a hockey game. Come see me when the game is over."

At 3:19 in the third period, Hayley picked up a loose puck and bolted towards the net. This was it; she was going to score. She was going to tie up the game. When the puck landed in the back of the net, she rushed towards her teammates for a quick celebration.

Then the Jayna–Vicky–Lori line took to the ice.

The teams squared up at centre ice. The puck dropped. Vicky won the faceoff and sent the puck over to Jayna. Jayna dug in and skated towards the net, firing off a hard shot. Just six seconds had passed on the clock. Again the puck sailed to the back of the net. Now it was 4–3. Canada had the lead!

The Canadians scored three more goals in the third period to win the game 7–3. The goals were scored by the "old guard." Vicky popped one in on a pretty pass from Danielle. Cassie scored a beautiful unassisted goal. Thérèse slapped one in with less than a minute on the clock.

After the game, Danielle said to a *Calgary Sun* reporter, "The old guys got it done."

And when Cheryl was asked about the previous USA dominance over Canada and if the eight losses were still in her mind, she replied, "It has happened. It's over. It's done."

To that Vicky smiled and piped up, "They weren't handing out medals in

The Old Guard

Thirty-six year old Danielle Goyette was the oldest member of the 2002 Olympic Women's Hockey Team. But when she mentioned the "old guys" in her quote, she was also referring to the team's veteran players. Next oldest on the team was Thérèse Brisson, who was thirty-five years old at the Games. She had played in the 1998 Olympics and in five World Championships. Geraldine Heaney was the only player on the team to play in seven World Championships. In 1990, at the first IIHF Women's World Championships tournament, she scored a TSN highlight goal. She retired from the team after the 2002 Olympics, at the age of thirty-four.

those games. A great quality in our team is believing in each other and not getting uptight."

It wasn't just the "old guard" who talked to the reporters. Rookie player Tammy spoke with confidence to the *Winnipeg Free Press*. "We went after them. I don't think a freight train would have stopped us."

But the biggest comment came from Hayley. So far she was leading the team in scoring. She was considered a veteran at the young age of twenty-four. Articles were written about her; that she was the best women's hockey player in the world. She was direct and honest with the *Winnipeg Free Press* when she said, "One thing with our team this year, it seems that with everything that seems to happen, it happens with adversity."

9 The Battle Begins

The gold–medal game was played on Thursday, February 22, 2002.

Cassie, Hayley, Danielle, Geraldine, and Thérèse were in charge of the *quote du jour*. The five players got together. They wanted to do something different, so they got now–famous Olympic Canadian figure skating pair Jamie Salé and David Pelletier to talk to the team.

Jamie and David told the Canadian women to go after their dreams and not to give up, no matter what. Look what had happened to them, they said. They had skated a flawless performance, yet had been awarded the silver medal. They knew they had done their best. The North American media didn't like the results and one of the judges admitted she had not been honest. Jamie and David had been given the gold medal. Their emotional talk, about doing the best they could, inspired the Canadian women.

Although they had arranged for Jamie and David to speak to the team, Cassie, Hayley, Thérèse, Geraldine, and Danielle still had their *quote du jour.*

When addressing the team, all they said was: "*Carpe Diem.*" This Latin expression means "Seize the Day!" or, in French, *Saisissez le Moment!*

That morning, Coach Danièle also left the players with some final words. "We will walk to the rink together, and when we are successful today, we will walk together forever. No one is allowed in our house today."

Coach Danièle talking to her team, keeping them focused.

When the Canadian women flew onto the ice, the stands were filled with plenty of Canadian fans wearing red and white, and lots of American fans wearing red, white, and blue.

The Canadian fans knew their team had recently lost eight in a row to the USA.

The American fans knew their team had a 35–0 record.

The warm-up for both teams was at a fast tempo. Earlier that morning, Kim had been told by Coach Danièle that she would be the starting goalie. After the tough semi-final game against the Finns, Danièle thought she was more prepared than the other goalies.

The puck dropped. Play began. And it was fast. Canada forechecked. Canada pressured. They played hard, aggressive hockey.

A thirty-second shift was all the players could handle. The game was too fast. They skated to the bench waving sticks. The next line was ready, eager to get on the ice and make this a game to remember.

One minute and forty-five seconds into the first period, Caroline, playing in her first Winter Olympics, saw a loose puck. First to the puck wins the battle, she knew. She raced to the puck. She pounced on it, picked it up, and fired it. When she saw it fly past the USA goalie, she screamed and jumped. Her teammates rushed over to her. Cherie picked up the assist. Two rookies had made that first goal happen.

Things looked good when the USA took a penalty at 6:17. But Canada didn't score on the power play. Then the USA took another penalty. Again for two minutes Canada tried to score. Canada's power play, once again, came out flat.

Then Jennifer took a tripping penalty. She skated to the box. The USA had a strong power play, but Canada had a strong

Kim St. Pierre getting in position to make a great glove save.

penalty kill. The penalty was almost over when Hayley took a delay-of-game penalty. The USA would have a five-on-three advantage for ten seconds.

The seconds ticked down. Canada killed one penalty. The gate opened, and Jennifer flew out of the box. The Canadians in the crowd cheered. Now the women just had to kill the rest of Hayley's penalty.

When Hayley finally returned to the game, the players pumped up the pressure. Five-on-five they were dominating the USA. They just had to stay out of the box.

Not even two minutes later, the referee put her arm up again. This time she pointed to Thérèse for bodychecking.

Players on the bench started talking about the penalties

"That wasn't a penalty."

"Why did she call that?"

Danielle, Jennifer, Dana, and Caroline hadn't played much in the past ten minutes. They weren't on the penalty-kill line. It was frustrating for them not to be able to play in such an important game, but they had to try to stay positive and keep team spirit up. They began to cheer loudly in support of their teammates.

When the referee put up her hand just

fifty-one seconds later, the Canadians groaned. Vicky got a two-minute penalty for cross-checking. The Canadians would again have to play for a minute with five-on-three.

Working hard, they killed both penalties.

When the buzzer sounded to end the period, the score was 1–0 for the Canadians.

They had played eight minutes out of twenty short-handed. To the crowd, the coaches, and the players, it seemed as if the American referee was making a lot of one-sided calls in favour of the home team.

The Canadians took to the ice in the second period determined to play five-on-five hockey. Five-on-five, they could win this game.

The puck dropped. The play started and went on for just over one minute. Then the referee put up her hand again. Becky was going to the box for hooking.

Yet again, the USA was going back on the power play.

Coach Danièle put out her first penalty-kill line. The USA moved the puck around in the Canadian zone. Back and forth. Finally, the defense rifled off a shot from the point. A USA player saw the puck and tipped it in. Kim didn't have a chance.

The USA had tied the game 1–1.

Back to five-on-five hockey, the Canadians refused to give up. Strong forechecking put the puck in the USA end. Danielle hadn't seen much ice in the first period. She wanted to do something. The loose puck was close. She picked it up and, on her backhand, sniped a shot at the USA goalie. Her shot was hard enough to send the rebound flying. On the blue line, Hayley saw the puck coming at her. Instead of waiting, she raced towards it. One stride, two strides . . . she was at the puck. With all her power, Hayley wound up and blasted a shot at the net. Hard and fast, the puck went high and straight upstairs, just under the crossbar.

At 2–1, the Canadians had reclaimed the lead.

Not even one minute later, the referee threw up her arm. She pointed to Caroline. Two minutes for roughing.

The Canadian crowd yelled that it was a cheap call. They were becoming extremely vocal about the number of penalties Canada was getting. Many were screaming at the referee.

Canada killed the penalty. Four minutes into the five-on-five the arm went up again. This time it was to Isabelle for tripping. With only a one-goal lead, Canada had to stay out of the box. But how, when the ref was calling everything?

Then Canada received yet another penalty less than a minute after Isabelle was out of the box, and the fans really screamed. As Jennifer skated to the box on a tripping call, Coach Danièle sent out her penalty-kill line.

Finally, the USA took a penalty. Canada went on the power play for over a minute. They cycled the puck; from wing to defense to wing to slot. The pressure was there, but the puck didn't make it past the USA goalie. When the USA penalty was

A New Olympic Sport

Women's hockey was introduced to the Winter Olympic Games in 1998 in Nagano, Japan. The United States won the gold medal, upsetting Canada 3-1. Players from the 2002 team who also played on the 1998 team were: Thérèse Brisson, Cassie Campbell, Geraldine Heaney, Becky Kellar, Jennifer Botterill, Lori Dupuis, Danielle Goyette, Janya Hefford, Vicky Sunohara, and Hayley Wickenheiser.

over, the game finally went back to five-on-five.

Canada felt more confident with the teams playing at even strength. Caroline rushed to the puck and battled. The USA player hammered at her. Then the referee blew her whistle. The USA would take a penalty and Canada would go on the power play.

But then the referee motioned for Caroline to go to the box, too. The USA had a roughing call and Canada, a holding call.

This was Canada's fifth penalty. They had played half the period short-handed.

The clock ticked down. Caroline and the USA player would have to sit in the box for the rest of the second period.

With only a few seconds left in the period, Jayna had the puck and saw an opening. She broke through and sent the puck past the USA goalie. She scored with just one second left on the clock!

When the buzzer sounded Canada went to the dressing room with a 3–1 lead.

10 Finishing Touches

The teams took to the ice for the third period. Not long in, the USA took a penalty. But then Canada took two back-to-back penalties. Becky got two minutes for roughing, and one minute after she was out of the box, Colleen got two minutes for bodychecking.

But the Canadians bore down and kept fighting. They iced the puck at every opportunity, forcing the USA players to skate to their own zone to pick it up. All the

Defense Cheryl Pounder works to tie a USA player up in front of the net so she can't score on Kim St. Pierre.

Canadians wanted to do was waste time.

If they could just keep their lead, they would win the gold.

With less then four minutes left in the game, the referee put her hand in the air. Canada touched the puck and the whistle blew. Kelly was going to the box for tripping.

The Canadian fans were irate. The American fans cheered.

The USA took possession of the puck off the faceoff. They set up in the Canadian end for their power play. The Canadian penalty-kill line hustled, trying to touch the puck. They needed to get it out and down the ice.

But the USA held on to the puck. They moved it around. The puck went back to a USA player at the point. A USA defense rifled a hard shot. It sailed past Kim and hit the back of the net.

The American fans went crazy.

With three minutes and thirty-three seconds left in the game, the USA was within one goal of catching Canada for a tie.

Everyone in the building knew that three minutes in hockey was a long time. There was still plenty of time for the USA to win the game. All it took was an unlucky bounce for the Canadians. The fans were on their feet. Fiery tension flamed through the arena. American fans yelled. Canadian fans yelled back.

On the bench, the Canadian players stayed calm. They still had the lead. They were still in the driver's seat.

Fans watched the clock. Players on the bench watched the clock.

The Canadians were so close. They just had to hold their lead.

Three minutes. Two minutes. The announcer made his "one minute left to play" call. The USA pulled their goalie. Six skaters against five. Canada had to hold on. They played with urgency, strength, and brains, but most of all, they played believing they could win this game.

When the final buzzer rang to end the gold-medal game in Salt Lake City, the Canadian Women's Hockey Team had won. They filled the arena with loud yells.

Forward Caroline Ouellette in front of the net putting the puck past the USA goalie.

Their arms were in the air. Gloves were tossed. Players mobbed one another.

The players skated around the rink, yelling and waving. Family members waved back, tears running down their faces. Canadian flags flew all over the arena.

The players draped the Canadian flag over their shoulders.

When the time came for the Canadian

flag to be raised, the Canadian Women's Hockey Team joined arm in arm. They rocked back and forth as they sang *O Canada* until their voices were hoarse.

11 *What a Story!*

The women stayed on the ice after the game, hugging and laughing and crying. Hayley brought her son on the ice and skated around holding him in her arms, kissing his forehead. With tear-stained faces and huge smiles, the players waved to their parents and friends in the crowd. They knew that family and friends had been there for them and had supported the team through their pre-Olympic struggle.

Instead of leaving the arena right after

With Canadian Flags draped around their shoulders, the Canadian Team and management staff line up to sing O Canada.

the game, the Canadian fans remained to watch the women. The game had been so dramatic. There had been so many penalties. Even the fans felt the emotional impact of the game and the tournament.

This team had overcome so much to win. They had had a rocky start, losing so many games. In Vancouver, after their eighth loss, when they could have given up, they had come together. They had cried then, too, but those weren't tears of joy. That had been their turning point. From that moment on, they believed that they could win and never wavered from their belief, despite what the critics said.

After the game, the media brought their cameras and microphones on to the ice. They wanted to talk to the players. This was a huge moment. Canada had broken their losing streak. After fifty years, hockey had come back and won an Olympic gold medal. The media slid

Kelly Béchard and Hayley Wickenheiser posing and having fun with their gold medals.

across the ice, hoping to get as many interviews as possible. The women were happy to talk.

When the *Toronto Star* approached Geraldine, she said, "Before the game, I was just thinking of how long I've played for the team; you know, winning seven world championships, a silver medal at the first Olympics...This is where I want it to end and to win a gold medal is perfect."

The players would miss Geraldine when she retired.

The captains of this team had worked so hard to keep the team together. The media lined up to speak with them. With her medal around her neck, Captain Cassie Campbell spoke to the *Toronto Star*. "Everything we've been through this year, it just seemed like what a story it's going to be, and I knew we were going to win."

Assistant Captain Hayley Wickenheiser also spoke to the *Toronto Star*. "It was very emotional. This team has been through a lot."

With a huge smile on her face, Vicky Sunohara told the *Toronto Sun*, "We had so much heart in our dressing room; we knew what we needed to do."

And they did know what they needed to do.

They needed to believe.

Epilogue

The women's stories spread in newspapers and magazines across Canada and in the USA. They were featured in *Maclean's, Time, The Hockey News*, and they even made *Sports Illustrated*.

The players became household names. This win raised interest in women's hockey. The sport now seemed to have more support from people all across Canada. Many were talking about how great women's hockey was to watch.

After coming home from Salt Lake City, rookie Kelly Béchard talked to her local paper, the *Saskatoon Leader Post*. "We faced a lot of adversity and had a lot of challenges that we had to overcome. We've had a lot of ups and downs over the last month. We've just gotten better and better every time we stepped on the ice. It got to the point where we didn't even question for a second if we could beat the Americans. I'm really excited to bring a gold medal back and see all my family and friends in Sedley and Regina. I know they've all been rooting for me and helping me all the way and it's going to be very special."

Another rookie, Colleen Sostorics, also told the *Saskatoon Leader Post*, "It's Canadian blood. We just know that when it counts we're going to come together and we're going to play as a team. It's kind of like you're pulling something from deep down inside you. It's one of the best feelings."

After the 2002 Olympics, registration across the country for women's hockey grew. Ontario saw the biggest jump. It went from 30,280 female hockey players in 2001–2002 to 34,710 in the season following the Salt Lake City Olympics. Another big jump was in Alberta. In 2001–2002, 5,137 girls were registered in the province to play hockey, and in 2002–2003 they saw that number increase to 6,882. In British Columbia, the numbers went from 4,741 in 2001–2002 to 5,321 the fall after the Olympic win. Most provinces recorded an increase in registration. Across the country, almost 7,000 more girls registered to play hockey in the fall after the 2002 Winter Olympics.

This rise in young girls playing hockey is good for the sport. It creates better players who know the game because they are starting younger. When they reach higher levels, they can play the fast tempo Olympic-style game. This gives Canadian coaches more players to choose from. It makes the National Team program have more depth.

The win the women had in 2002 also gave young girls many role models. Years ago female hockey players looked to the male players as role models. Now, young girls look to female hockey players.

When Cheryl Pounder heard that six million television viewers had watched the game she told the Canadian Press, "We have changed the face of women's hockey."

Hayley Wickenheiser now runs a tour of cross-Canada hockey clinics for female players. "We really are very serious about being role models for young girls," she says.

Cassie Campbell has gone on to become a broadcaster for Hockey Night in

Canada. She runs a ball hockey tournament in Calgary, Alberta, to raise money for Ronald McDonald House. The tournament is extremely well attended because of her fame from winning an Olympic gold medal. Many other players also run hockey camps that have become popular for young girls in the summer.

It has also become socially acceptable for girls to sign up for hockey. It used to be that parents didn't want their girls playing hockey because they didn't think girls should play such a rough sport. But now girls sign up because their parents have watched the Olympics and seen how great a sport it is for women.

Young girls playing hockey now have something to strive for. They can try to excel and become National Team players. "Now, young girls have the Olympics," said Hayley. "That's our Stanley Cup."

Glossary

Breakaway: A player in full control of the puck, and having no opposing player between them and the other team's goalie or net.

Cross-checking: Using the shaft of the stick between the two hands to check an opponent at any height.

Cycling the puck: Passing the puck from player to player in the other team's zone. Players do this to try and create a clear opening to score. Usually, they pass the puck quite quickly.

Even strength or five-on-five: When both teams have all five players plus their goalies on the ice at the same time.

Faceoff: The action of the referee dropping the puck between the sticks of two opposing players to start or resume play.

High sticking: Carrying the stick or any part of the stick above the normal height of the shoulder.

Holding: When a player uses her hands on an opponent or the opponent's equipment to stop the opponent's progress.

Hooking: Using the blade of the stick in a pulling or tugging motion to stop an opponent.

Minor penalty: For a minor penalty, a player is sent off the ice for two minutes of actual playing time.

One-timing: Passing the puck to a teammate who immediately shoots the puck without stopping it first.

Penalty kill: A team with a player in the penalty box has to try to play short-handed and not let the other team score on them. If they are successful then they are said to have "killed the penalty."

Penalty: The result of an infraction to the rules.

Point: When a team is trying to score and they are in their opponent's zone, the area near the blue line and the boards is called "the point." Usually, the defense players position themselves on the point.

Power play: When a team is playing with all their players on the ice against a team that is short one player due to a penalty. The team with more players has the advantage and they are "on the power play."

Slashing: Hitting an opponent with the stick while holding the stick with one or both hands.

Slot: The area on the ice which is directly ahead of the goaltender between the faceoff circles on each side. This can be referred to as the "scoring area" as well.

Stood-on-her-head: The term used when a goalie stops shot after shot from her opposition and doesn't let the puck go in the net.

Unanswered goal: Scoring more than one goal in a row without the other team scoring in between.

Acknowledgements

It takes a supportive crowd to write a Recordbook. I would like to thank André Brin, Aaron Wilson, and Jennifer Robins at Hockey Canada for providing me with photos and information on this team. I would also like to thank all the players who responded to my e-mails, the ones where I asked a ton of questions. I so appreciate your time and energy. Sami Jo Small put together the most amazing scrapbook of this team's journey to the Olympics and it was like a precious stone to me as it gave me insight into each player and to the tournament. Carrie Gleason, my editor at Lorimer, was patient and insightful with her edits. I thank her and the Lorimer team. And finally, I would like to thank my husband, Bob Nicholson, because without him I would not have attended the 2002 Winter Olympics, nor would I have been able to watch these amazing women win their gold medal. I was lucky to be there as a fan, and I knew that it was a great story worth telling.

About the Author

Lorna Schultz Nicholson is a full-time writer in Calgary, Alberta, where she lives with her husband, Hockey Canada President Bob Nicholson, and their three children. She is the author of a fiction hockey series in the Lorimer Sports Stories, including *Too Many Men* which was nominated for the Diamond Willow award. Lorna is the author of *Pink Power* and *Fighting for Gold* in the Recordbooks series.

Photo Credits

Thanks to Hockey Canada for providing all of the photos, including front and back cover, for this book.

Index

More gripping underdog tales of sheer determination and talent!

● RECORDBOOKS

Recordbooks are action-packed true stories of Canadian athletes who have changed the face of sport. Check out these titles available at bookstores or your local library, or order them online at www.lorimer.ca.